Order Bride

Ninph Blick

Contents

Chapter 1

C hapter 1

It had taken Anna almost four years to realize that she'd made the stupidest decision of her life. Yup, she'd moved to New York. A country girl in the city what a sight.

The first couple of years she thought that she could make it, but last year money had gotten extremely tight and Anna almost had to go crawling back home to her parents not like they would accept her anymore. She'd left for the city and now she was a disappointment.

Her plan was to move back to the country, just not the small town she had come from. The only problem was which one and where would it be?

Anna hadn't talked to her best friend Chrissie yet. She would be so devastated when she would find out that Anna was leaving. Chrissie was the first person she had met upon her arrival in the city, and they'd just hit it off. If her parents saw Chrissie they'd probably shake their heads and walk the other way.

Chrissie was your average punk rocker girl. She had her hair half normal color and then every couple weeks it would be a different color. Sometimes it was brown and blue, other times it was brown and orange. Honestly it just depended on her mood.

Living in the city was starting to get depressing. Anna needed out and fast. Maybe until she could figure something out, she could just go and get a pint of ice cream and some magazines. It had been her cure all in the past and it still worked now.

Anna walked down the busy New York street to her favorite book store. They had a full row of magazines and it was like heaven to Anna when she was in a mood. She entered the store and walked directly over to the magazine rack.

Times like this called for the current Vogue, Esquire, and maybe the new Vanity Fair. Oh God, was that a copy of Playboy, ewww. Anna never understood why males found those magazines so interesting. Well she did but males were such perverts that it really didn't matter. She'd had a brother so she knew what they contained, but really, it was still gross.

As she cowered the racks to look for other magazines she might indulge in she came across one with pictures of cowboys across the front and it said, "Western Love." It had ads in it for country boys and cowboys looking for love.

She was intrigued by the magazine. Maybe this was her way out of the city. Anna couldn't wait until she could get back to her apartment and read the whole thing. There had to be a man in it that she could find to help her out of this mess she called life.

Anna walked over to the cashier and handed him the magazines. "Ma'am that will be fifteen dollars and twelve cents, please." She handed the man a twenty and waited for her change. "Have a nice day," he said.

"Thanks." With that she was out the door and she decided she still wanted a pint of ice cream, so she quickly stopped at the corner store near her apartment. After she'd completed her purchase she walked around the corner to her apartment. Her apartment was only one bedroom she couldn't really afford anything bigger on her tiny editor salary, but her part was rather nice if she did say so herself.

Anna worked at a newspaper company as an editor, she'd gone to college for writing but that hadn't panned out so she'd fallen back on editing. It paid the bills, but it also bored her. All she did was check grammar and she loathed it. She wanted to be the one writing these articles not checking to see if there were any errors.

It took a couple minutes to get past the bell hop to the elevator. She would have been up to her apartment sooner, but there was a crowd of people and only one elevator, and Anna really didn't feel like walking up fifteen flights of stairs. So she'd waited and got stuck on an elevator with a man talking about his next big Wall Street deal. The man was annoying and Anna was tempted to tell him to shut up and shove it.

Anna just about ran out of the elevator when the doors opened and made her way to 15E. Home sweet home, she thought. She grabbed a spoon and then collapsed on her couch with her ice cream and magazines.

First she grabbed the copy of Western Love. She read through all the ads, but she kept finding herself going back to this one ad. The man was hot she could tell that under his chambray shirt he had some seriously defined pecks and broad, broad shoulders, that screamed of manual labor. The man was hot and his eyes intrigued her. They were a gorgeous smoky gray color. His skin was tanned to perfection for the long days he'd obviously spent out on the range.

She liked his ad even though it was so simple and straight forward. She liked how if she was to send him a letter she'd probably get a straight forward no bullshit answer.

Brent Donovan

Age: 29

Lives in Walker, Montana, he's ready to find to find that special girl that he can spend the rest of his days with. He grew up on his family's ranch. His spread is currently seven thousand acres and growing every day. Brent enjoys riding the range and herding cattle. He's your average good ol' cowboy. If you decide to send him a letter your life will never be boring. You don't want to miss out on this one girl's.

To send him a letter, or not to?

If Chrissie was with her right now she'd probably think her crazy for even considering sending this cowboy a letter. Oh how she wanted to, but it was a little out there even for her. She'd sleep on the idea and if she still wanted to send him a letter then she'd do it after she talked to Chrissie at work.

She went into her room and immediately went to sleep. Her dreams were filled with one hot and sexy cowboy that intrigued her.

*****

When she woke up the next morning she felt refreshed. Her first thoughts were about Brent. She wondered what his life was like and what he was doing right now. She had to push those thoughts from her brain and get ready for work. She had to be on the other side of town in a little over an hour and she was nowhere near ready.

She jumped in the shower for a quick shower and then put her hair up in a slightly messy bun. She put on a pair of jeans with her equestrian riding boots. For her shirt she decided to put on a plaid shirt and she grabbed her brown leather jacket. She looked good if she did say so herself.

Anna grabbed her bag and an apple and then she was out the door, getting ready to head towards the subway. She almost dreaded going into work today because she was going to have to tell Chrissie that she was going to be leaving soon. Well that was if everything worked out after she sent Brent a letter.

The subway was packed just like every other morning. She managed to find a seat next a rather friendly couple if you know what she meant, but it was a seat and she really didn't feel like standing the whole time.

They pulled into her stop, and she stood up quickly ready to get away from the couple.

She had fifteen minutes to make it to work, and if the streets were just as busy as they usually were then she would have no problem making it to work on time.

If there was one thing she hated about the city was how busy and congested the streets were. Did people not know what it was like to take their time, and not have to be in a rush? Obviously not. She couldn't wait to get out of here and live life at a slower pace.

When she got to the building she worked in se sighed, another day of boring work. She got on the elevator and pressed seven waiting for the elevator to come to a stop at her floor. She had to push her way past the rest of the people to get out of the elevator.

Her cubby was on the far side of the office so she quickly maneuvered her way around all the cubby's to make it to hers.

Chrissie was waiting for her. "Why didn't you call me last night like you said you would?" she asked expectantly.

She'd forgotten about that. "Oh, sorry I went and got a couple of maga-zines, and I fell asleep reading them."

Chrissie rolled her eyes. Whenever there was something wrong with her friend she would read magazines and eat ice cream. "Sure and let me guess there was some ice cream involved in this too? Of course there was." Chrissie sighed. "What's wrong?"

"I don't know I guess I'm just tired of living in the city. I thought I would love it when I got here, but it's been almost five years and I hate it."

Chrissie faked a pout. "You don't like your best friend." She gasped.

She swatted her hand at Chrissie. "Oh, Chrissie stop being so dramatic, you know I can't stand this place, not you. You're the best thing that has happened to me since I got here."

"Yeah, yeah."

"One of the magazines I got was filled with ads by guys that want to find a significant other-"

Chrissie interrupted her. "You can't tell me your seriously considering this? What if these guys are psycho killers."

Anna sighed. "First off Chrissie they wouldn't let them have ads in these if they were, and there's this one that intrigues me. He name is Brent Donovan-"

Once again Chrissie interrupted her. "Do you have it with you?" Anna nodded yes. "Can I see it?"

Anna grabbed it out of her bag and handed it to her. "It reminds me off mail order brides..." She paused. "What do you think of him?"

"He's hot."

"Yeah I know. Should I send him a letter?"

"Sure. He seems like he's nice and straight forward, just how you like them." She shrugged. "It's your life do whatever you want."

"I was going to send him a letter. I just wanted to get your opinion first." Anna looked to the left oh crap! The boss was approaching them. "You might want to go back to your cubby," she said pointing to the left. "I'll call you tonight."

"Okay." Chrissie crossed over to her cubby quickly.

Both of them began to work fast. Their boss Jenkins passed by them and said, "I don't pay you to gossip, or whatever ladies. I want to see you both working. You will both have to edit five more articles now." He really was an unpleasant person.

They both inwardly groaned and nodded. He seemed to be satisfied by their nods and so he walked away.

The rest of the day passed by rather uneventfully, Anna had lunch with Chrissie. Chrissie avoided the topic of Anna leaving as if it was the plague.

When Anna got home that night she ordered some pasta from an Italian bistro around the corner from her building. After she'd changed into some sweats she booted up her computer and began to compose the letter she was going to send Brent.

Dear Brent Donovan,

I saw your ad and I decided that I would send you a letter. My name is Anna Douglas I'm twenty-seven, and I currently live in New York City. Now don't let that fool you I was raised in a small town in Georgia. I am very much so a small town girl. My parents own a small farm and a store in town. After I finished college I decided to move to the city to pursue my career, I currently work at a newspaper as an editor.

Honestly I hate living in the city and I would like to move back to a small town, but I don't want to go back home. The other day I saw your ad in that magazine, and I thought to myself, he's perfect.

I would have no problem fitting in on your ranch or in your town. As I said I'm twenty-seven and I've decided that I'd like to move into the next stage of my life which means finding a significant other. I hope that's not too straight forward. One thing you'll find out about me is that I don't like to beat around the bush. If you do decide to send me a letter back I'd be overjoyed. Also I think you'd like me if you ever get the chance to get to know me. Thank you for taking time out of your busy day to read this.

P.S. There is a picture of myself enclosed as well

Sincerely Yours,

Anna Douglas

She enclosed the letter in an envelope, and set it aside. She's send it tomorrow before she went to work.

Her doorbell chimed alerting her that her food was here. She grabbed a twenty out of her wallet and walked to the door. The delivery man was waiting on the other side of her door as she'd expected. She paid him quickly and then closed the door.

Anna went into her kitchen to get a glass of wine and a fork. The heavenly aroma of pesto chicken pasta wafted past her nose and her mouth watered. This was the best pasta she had ever had in her life.

After dinner Anna decided she'd better call Chrissie. She dialed her number which she knew by heart. After two rings Chrissie answered. "Hey, did you write the letter?"

"Uh, yeah it's in an envelope sitting by my purse ready to be sent."

Chrissie sighed. "I don't want you to leave me. How will I survive, especially at work, you know how Jenkins is."

"You will be fine he's not that bad. Plus it will get better for you when you and I are not talking all the time while we're supposed to be working."

"I guess you're right, but promise me one thing?"

Anna couldn't help but wonder what she was going to ask her. "Yeah?"

"Promise me we'll visit each other rather often. I don't care if it's you coming to visit me or me visiting you."

"Of course you're my best friend; I'll always want to be near you."

The rest of the conversation flowed easily, there was no more strain from Anna's upcoming departure. She went to sleep that night feeling happy with the decision she'd made. In the morning she'd send Brent her letter and hope for the best.

Chapter 2

So I avoided doing some of my other work so that I could get this chapter up. Anna and Brent speak for the first time in this chapter, but it's only over the phone. Don't worry hopefully in the next chapter they will meet! I feel like the song on the side describes Anna pretty well. I hope you enjoy this chapter!!! Please vote and comment if you liked the chapter!

Chapter 2

Brent couldn't believe he'd let his sister convince him to put an ad in that magazine. He prayed that no one read it magazine and would send him a letter. He didn't want some city girl coming and trying to fit in on his ranch. The William D. Ranch was no place for some wimpy city girl.

The letters had been coming in like crazy for a week. Honestly when Brent had let Cassie, his sister, convince him to put in an ad, he'd thought he'd get maybe one or two replies. Nope his kitchen table was stacked with letter upon letter from desperate females. Great!

Yeah, not really, Brent just hoped that no one else would reply to the ad. As it was he wasn't going reply to any of the dozens of letters he'd received. Brent read a couple of the letters but no of them appealed to him, it seemed as if some of the women were only after him for his land. It would be a cold day in hell when he married someone who only wanted him for his land. He didn't care how mad Cassie got at him. It just simply wasn't going to happen, he was going to put his foot down and end this whole thing.

When Brent got home from working on the ranch later that day he grabbed the stack of mail, and before he realized what he was doing he'd ended up reading a letter from someone who had seen his ad. This Anna person seemed very interesting. She wasn't really a city girl she'd been raised on a farm, and if her picture was any indication then she was very attractive. Maybe, one of these females could fit in here.

Brent called for Cassie to come and immediately regretted doing that. "What big brother?" She yelled as she walked down the hallway to their living room.

He was cursing himself under his breath for calling Cassie out here. "Uh, nothing sorry I didn't mean to call you out here."

She grinned at him. "Yup, sure big brother and my real names not Cassandra." She looked up at him with a curious expression on her face. "What's going on, does it have something to do with that letter in your hand?"

"Uh, no."

She could always tell when he was lying. "Are you lying to me?" She took a step towards him. "Let me see the letter."

He had to give up some time and let her see the letter so he decided now was as good a time as any. "Fine." He handed her the letter.

Cassie spent a few seconds reading the letter and then looking at the picture. 'She's really pretty, and she's looking for a way out of the city and back to the country. I'd say this is a win, win situation for both of you. Why don't you send her a letter back?"

She was graced with a one worded reply. "No."

"Why not she's perfect?"

Brent sighed. "No Cassie I agreed to put the ad out there but I did not agree to bring one of these females here."

"Come on Brent you're lonely and we both know it."

He rubbed his and across his face as if he was trying relieve some of his stress. "Cassie when I decide to get married it will be with someone I know and love."

"Okay so bring her here, get to know her and then fall in love with her.it never hurts to try, and if it doesn't work out then just send her back."

"Oh, little sister you may be twenty-five but you are very small minded. You and I both know that love doesn't work that way."

Cassie sighed in frustration. "But it could if you'd just give it a try."

"No."

She smiled smugly. "Fine if you won't send her a letter, then I will."

"Oh, no you won't"

"Oh, yes I will. That is unless you send her a letter first. I'm not giving up on this."

He threw his arms up in defeat. "Fine I'll send her a letter. Are you happy now?"

Brent walked away mumbling something about how he hoped this wouldn't ruin his life. Cassie just smiled and called after him. "Since you I asked, I am happy now."

As Brent walked into his office, he realized that he should have given in to Cassie so easily. Now he had to write a letter he didn't want to write, and to someone he didn't even know.

Well, he did kind of want to get know her. Who wouldn't, she was a knockout.

He sat down at his large maple desk that faced the living room. There wasn't much décor in his home that didn't have so sort of country or western flair to it.

That was another reason why he didn't want to bring a female there. They would try and change everything about his life. First it would be adding just a "little" to his décor, and then it would be the way he dressed; which he didn't seen anything wrong with. Then she would have him by the balls and be able to drag him around like a puppy dog. That sure as hell wasn't going to happen.

For god's sake he was an extremely wealthy rancher who did whatever the hell he pleased, and no woman, and he meant it was going to change that. Well that's what he hoped at least. How was he supposed to know what the future would bring?

Dear Anna,

I received your letter earlier today. I felt like I should write you and thank you for sending me a letter. There are a few things about me I feel like I should let you know. I have a younger sister named Cassandra, but I call her Cassie for short. She is the one who convinced me to put an ad in that magazine. To tell you the truth if it hadn't been for her I would not be sending you this letter back.

So with that out of the way I would like to invite you to come to my home in Montana. I don't know if something between you and I will work out, but we can give it a try, and if it doesn't then no harm, no foul. I will be inclosing my personal phone numbers in this letter. I would like it if you could call me whenever you get this letter so that we can work out all the details of you coming here. If you've changed your mind then as I said before no harm, no foul.

Sincerely,

Brent

Brent read over the letter a couple of times and decided that it was good enough. He printed it off and then sent it with one of the hands that was going into town tonight so it could be mailed. Maybe this would work, maybe it wouldn't, who knows?

*****

It had been almost a week since Anna had sent Brent the letter. She was beginning to wonder if she would receive a letter back. He'd probably had tons and tons of women send him letters, he was a catch, just one look at him and any women could tell that.

She was daydreaming about a guy she didn't even know at work. Anna really should get back to editing before Jenkins would come by for his afternoon check. She really did not like that man. No matter how many times she had told Chrissie that he wasn't that bad she had yet to convince herself he wasn't so bad.

"Pssss." Anna looked around trying to figure out who was trying to get her attention. She immediately knew it was Chrissie when she looked at her.

"What are you daydreaming about?" She asked as she looked at her expec-tantly.

Anna twirled a pen between her fingers as she spoke. "That guy Brent." She signed. "It's been a week since I sent him a letter and I'm wondering if he received it or if he's ignoring it."

Chrissie should have known she was thinking about Brent. There hadn't been much time this past week when Anna hadn't been thinking about him. "I don't think that any guy is so much of an asshole that he'd just over look a letter especially when he put the ad in that magazine in the first place.

Anna considered what Chrissie had said for a moment. "Maybe your right, he could still send me a letter. Who knows maybe when I get to my apartment there will be a letter in my box from him."

Chrissie smiled, glad that her friend was thinking on the bright side. "There's that positive attitude. Just keep being positive and hopefully everything will work out."

"You're right once again."

She smiled at Anna triumphantly. "Don't you just love it when I'm right?"

Anna chucked the pen that was still in her hands at Chrissie. "Hey why'd you do that?"

Anna couldn't help but laugh, which caused quite a few eyes to look her direction. "You didn't have to be so cocky about it."

Later that day after she'd gotten home from work she was shuffling through her mail when she came across a letter with handwriting she wasn't familiar with. A closer inspection told her that is was from Brent, and when she saw that letter her breathe caught in her throat.

So he had replied. He hadn't for gotten about her letter. Somehow she felt triumphant. To tell you the truth she hadn't put much faith in getting a reply back because who knew if he'd chosen someone else.

She tore through the letter fast. It was only one page, but that didn't mean anything he could have condensed everything he'd wanted to say in that letter. She read the letter once and then to reconfirm what she'd read, she read it a couple more times.

Anna collapsed on the couch. He'd probably received dozens of letters, but he'd chosen her. He wanted her to come to Montana. She felt so happy; the sexy cowboy had chosen her. Not anyone else, but her.

Her excitement came out while she jumped and danced around her apartment with glee. He'd left his phone numbers at the bottoms of the page so that she could call and they could figure out all the details. Once she'd calmed down some she'd calm him.

About fifteen minutes later she'd calmed down immensely and had decided that it was time to call Brent. She was shaking as she dialed the first number, her nerves were coming out. The phone rang once, and then twice, and then someone picked up the phone.

"Hello?" The person on the other side said expectantly.

"Hello, this is Anna, Anna Douglas."

"Oh, hello Anna it's me Brent." His voice was deep and sexy. Anna immediately loved it.

"I just got your letter. I thought that we could talk about me coming to Montana."

He sighed which she thought was weird because he was the one who'd invited her to come to Montana. "Oh yes, I'm glad you've decided to take me up on my offer. I was wondering how soon you could be here?"

"I'm not sure, I wasn't sure if I'd get a reply back so I haven't put my two weeks' notice in, but I can do that as soon as tomorrow. I also need to pack up my apartment and get rid of some of my stuff."

He was going to regret this. "You can bring some of your furniture and décor with you. We can get a storage unit in town and start integrating some of your stuff into my house." He couldn't believe he'd just suggested that when just a couple days ago he'd told himself that he wouldn't let any woman change anything about his life.

What was it about this woman? Just listening to her sweet voice had him in a trance.

"That would be wonderful." He could hear the smile in her voice. It gave him some pleasure knowing that he'd made her smile.

He cleared his throat. "So you said that you still had to give your two weeks' notice, right?" He asked.

"Yes."

"So if I get you a plane ticket for two and a half weeks from now, do you think that would be enough time to pack up your stuff and finish up with your job?"

Anna was so happy everything was working out "I think that that would be the perfect amount of time for me to get everything done, but one question what's your address. I need to know so that I can get my things shipped to your house."

He told her his address and she quickly wrote it down. "I've got to go, but I'll call you once I have your plane ticket set up."

"Okay." As Brent was getting ready to hang up Anna spoke again urgently. "Brent?"

"Yeah."

Anna sighed. "I just wanted to say thank you for picking me. It really means a lot."

He didn't really know how to reply to that. "No problem I'll talk to you later. Bye."

"Bye." They both disconnected the phones at the same time.

Once Anna was off the phone she began to get boxes out for packing and draft her two weeks' notice letter. All she knew was that this was going to be a long two and a half weeks.

Chapter 3

H ere's the next chapter, I hope you enjoy! Please comment and vote! Thanks!

Chapter 3

Jenkins accepted her two weeks' notice which Anna was happy about. She did feel guilty when she handed in her notice. She was leaving Chrissie here to survive by herself. It also really hit her hard that she was getting to leave the city when she handed in her notice.

For the past couple of days Anna had been packing nonstop. She'd gotten rid of a lot stuff, but she'd also kept a lot because she just couldn't part with some of her belongings.

She only had a little under two weeks left to go. Besides packing a ton Anna had been spending a ton of time with Chrissie before she had to leave.

Last night Brent had called her with the details with her flight and the shipping of her stuff. They'd chatted a little bit, but it had seemed like he hadn't really wanted to talk too much so she'd made an excuse to get off the phone after talking for about ten minutes.

Anna was excited to meet Brent in person. He seemed like a great guy, she could get used to spending time with him. She liked talking with him just from their two short conversations. Although he'd seemed kind of reserved like he didn't exactly want to talk to her, but then again maybe she was just imagining it.

As she was packing she found a box in the bottom of her closet. It was filled with little things she'd kept to help her remember her family. She hadn't talked to them in a little over five years. As soon as she'd announced she was moving to the city they'd disowned her.

The scars from their disapproval were still raw, and whenever she thought about them not wanting her anymore she fought to keep the tears at bay. She couldn't leave they'd just disowned her. Weren't you supposed to love your children? Obviously her parents had missed that little piece of information.

It wasn't like she'd been trying to forget about her country roots. The only reason she had moved to the city was that she'd hoped that she could kick start her career which she couldn't really do where she was from. Her parents hadn't wanted to listen to reason though. They heard the word 'city' and then she meant nothing to them.

What hurt the most was that she hadn't seen her little brother. She missed him so much, Jake was everything to her. Her parents refused to let him talk to her when she'd first left but he was now twenty-four and every once in a while she would get a letter or a postcard from him. Most of the time they just told her that he was doing well and that he missed her. No matter how bad she wanted to reply to them she had to refrain from doing so because if her parents found out he was speaking to her then they'd disown him too, and Anna wouldn't be able to live with herself if that happened.

While she was going through the box she found a picture from Jake's first birthday party, she was standing next to him and both of their faces were covered in chocolate cake. It was the perfect picture.

After she finished looking at the picture she put it up and carried the box into the living room. She tried to pack some more so that she could avoid thinking about her family. She missed them so much, but she just had to push through it and think about all the good things she currently had in her life.

*****

The last of Anna's time in New York had come to an end; she'd finished her last day of work a couple days ago. They'd thrown her a little going away party with a really cute cake. Chrissie was the only person who knew why Anna was going to Montana. Her old coworkers just thought that she was going home to be with her family.

Anna hadn't slept much last night. She tossed and turned thinking about Brent and his sister. He hadn't really said anything about Cassie, but she was excited to meet her. Chrissie was going to be going to the airport with her today. She'd had most of her stuff shipped to Montana a couple days ago so it should arrive shortly after she does.

They arrived at the airport a couple hours before Anna's flight was scheduled to leave. It was going to be hard to say bye to Chrissie. Currently Chrissie was the only family that Anna had, and even though it was breaking her heart to leave she knew she had to do this for herself.

As they walked towards the security there was an awkward silence in the air. Chrissie broke the silence first. "I don't care what you do there, okay I do, but just get too busy that you can't call or Skype your best friend."

Anna couldn't help but smile at Chrissie, she really was going to miss her. "I won't forget. How could I, I'm your best friend?"

"If this guy is a douche bag don't be afraid to come back." Chrissie said seriously.

"It'll be fine I've told you he's a really nice guy. Plus you know how I feel about the city."

"Okay." Chrissie's eyes started to get misty. "I don't want to say goodbye to you."

She Chrissie close to tears almost undid Anna. "Neither do I. This is going to be one of the hardest things I've ever had to do."

Chrissie gripped her tightly in a bear hug. "I love you Anna you're like the sister I never had."

Big tears were rolling down Anna's face as she spoke. "Ah, I love you, too. I'm going to miss you so much. We will always be best friend and sisters even if were not really related." Anna tried to wipe away her tears but it was no use they were falling to fast for her do anything about them.

Through their tears they both smiled at each other. Anna looked at her watch and saw that she needed to get through security soon so that she wouldn't miss her flight. "Well, I guess this is goodbye. You don't forget about me either, okay?" She gripped Chrissie closer.

"I won't. Bye." She wiped at her tears as well.

"I guess I better get going." Anna hugged Chrissie one more time.

"I'll see you later. Call me when you get there."

"Okay, see yah." They both parted ways. Anna couldn't wait until she would see Chrissie again, and she had the feeling that Chrissie felt the same way.

Security took a little over twenty minutes to get through. Her terminal was on the other side of the airport so she had to take the little train to terminal C.

There were fast food places, but Anna had already eaten that morning so she just bypassed them and went to her gate. She had a half an hour before her flight arrived so she grabbed her laptop out of her bag and began to work on one of the stories she'd been working on. She wanted to try and get some of them published. It was a dream of hers.

A few minutes they called all the passengers for boarding. "Can all the people on Flight 863 to Helena, Montana come to gate C29, your flight is now boarding."

Anna packed up her laptop and walked over to the gate. She handed the lady her ticket and boarded the plane. She managed to find an empty row so she scooted in and took the window seat. She loved being able to look out the window when she flew.

Soon the plane was taxying down the runway, preparing to take off. Anna hadn't slept much last night because the nerves had kept her awake. Once the plane was in the air she adjusted her seat and the pillow that she had gotten from the flight attendant, so that she could try and sleep some during the sic hour flight. Anna managed to finally fall asleep about an hour into the flight.

"Please refasten your seat belt and move your trays into the up position. We are preparing for landing." This is what Anna woke up to. She yawned and moved around to get comfortable for landing.

Within minutes the plane was at the gate and people were beginning to get off the flight. Anna was one of the last people to get off the plane. The other night when Anna had talked to Brent he'd told her that he'd be waiting for her at baggage carousel A. Now she only had to figure out where that was. Simple, right?

Not so much the airport was huge. She ended up getting turned around and going the opposite direction of the carousel. Finally after getting help from someone at the airport, she was headed in the right direction, towards baggage carousel A.

Anna looked around trying to see if she could see Brent, but there were so many people that it was hard to look for him. Maybe if she waited a minute and got her luggage then the carousel might clear out some so that she could find Brent.

It took Anna a while to locate her checked bags. When she was about to move to the side to look for Brent, someone touched her arm. Curious as to whom it was she turned around and was graced for the first time with Brent's face in person. She smiled a dazzling smile at him. That picture didn't do him justice; he was so handsome it took her breath away.

"Anna?" He spoke tentatively as if he wasn't sure it was her

She smiled at him once again and moved in for a hug. "It's so nice to finally meet you."

Yeah, it is. Are these your bags?" He asked pointing at the two large suitcases standing next to her.

"Yeah, I'm so excited to be here. I can't wait to meet your sister and get to see your ranch."

He didn't respond to her and she wondered why he wasn't talkative. They started to walk towards the exit to the parking lot. He was wheeling her suitcases along for her.

"Brent I can wheel my suitcases around if you'd like?" She asked.

He seemed to be agitated by what she had said. "It's fine. I brought you here, the least I can do is wheel your suitcases around."

Well, then she hadn't been expecting that at all. From then on silence was the norm between them. He loaded her things into the bed of his truck. Sometimes Anna would ask questions about Montana, but he would give her strained answers, so she just gave up trying to make conversation. Safe to say the three hour ride to William D. Ranch was very tense and awkward.

Anna had fallen asleep for most of the last hour of the ride but she was awoken by a rather large bump in the road.

When they passed through the gate Brent said, "Home sweet, home."

She yawned and looked around. It was beautiful, it was late enough that the sun was beginning to set. Anna hadn't thought about how Montana would be or look, but right now with the view she had it was breathtaking.

She was awestruck by Montana's beauty. "Your land is beautiful, when I lived in Georgia with my parents on their farm it looked nothing like this."

He gave her a half smile. "Welcome to William D. Ranch, Anna."

She could get the huge smile she had on off her face. "Thanks."

Brent just shrugged. They pulled into the drive of an enormous log cabin ranch house. "This will be your new home Anna. Do you like it?"

She scoffed. "Like it, I love it. I've always wanted to live in a house that looks just like this one."

"I'm glad to hear it." He motioned her to the house with his hand. Let's go inside, Cassie has been looking forward to meeting you." He looked around the spacious living room, but Cassie was nowhere in sight. "Cassie we're home." He bellowed.

A pretty girl a couple years younger than Anna came walking into the living room. Her hair was the same shade of brown as Brent's, but instead of having smoky gray eyes like her brother they were more of a chocolate brown color. She was rather petit with nice curves.

Cassie ran over and gave Anna a hug. "I'm glad you're here." She looked over at her brother. "I hope he's been a perfect gentleman. My parents and I tried to teach him manners but were-☐

Brent glared at Cassie. "Cassandra Nicole Donovan."

Cassie smiled sheepishly at Anna. "Looks like I'm in trouble."

A smile spread across Anna's face, she was going to enjoy spending time with these two. "Don't worry Cassie he was the perfect gentleman."

At that Cassie giggled. "Are you sure about that?"

Brent just rolled his eyes. "I'm going to go and get Anna's suitcases out of the truck, while you two finish chatting." He turned to walk away, but then he remembered something. "Oh and Cassie can you please show Anna which room she will be staying in, please?"

"Sure no problem." The two continued two chat like they were old friends.

The room that they had designated for Anna was located on the second floor, down the hall from Brent's room and next door to Cassie's.

Anna and Cassie walked into the room. "I tried to spruce it up a bit." Cassie said. "But feel free to decorate it however you with."

The room was rather big. In the middle of the far wall there was a queen bed and on the right side there as a reading chair with a built in book case next to it. There were two dressers in the room and one had a mirror on it. The room was bigger than the one Anna had had in New York so she was sure that she'd be more than fine living in it.

"I'll be sure to do that when my things get here."

"Well I'll be going know." Cassie crossed to the door preparing to exit.

"I think I'm just going to turn in for the night." Anna said. "I've had a long day with the flight and the drive here."

"Okay, I'll tell Brent so he's quite when he brings your suitcases up."

"Thanks, I'll see you in the morning." Once Cassie was gone Anna crawled into bed, exhausted from the day's activities.

Chapter 4

I'm sorry for not getting another chapter up sooner. I've had some family issues and I also had to put my dog down today. Safe to say it hasn't been the best week.

You will be meeting a new character in this chapter. I felt like I had to give Cassie a beau, the picture on the side is of Clint. I hope you enjoy! Please comment and vote!

Chapter 4

A light streaming through Anna's window woke her up the next morning. Looking at her alarm clock she realized that it was half past seven in the morning. She never slept in that late during the week. She must really have been exhausted the night before.

Grudgingly she got out of bed and went to go take a shower in the bathroom across the hall. Afterwards she felt rejuvenated and ready to take on the world. She made it down stairs at a quarter past eight and much too her surprise both Cassie and Brent were in the kitchen eating breakfast.

"Good morning, I'm glad you're awake. I didn't want to wake you up because I figured you'd still be tired from yesterday." Cassie said.

"Thanks I was, but nothing that a good night's sleep couldn't fix." Anna inhaled and hit with the mouthwatering aromas of whatever they were eating. "Wow, something smells delicious."

Brent looked up from his paper. "There are some fresh cinnamon rolls in the kitchen. Feel free to help yourself."

"Okay." Anna made her way to the kitchen and as she was about to grab a plate when she realized she had no clue where they were.

Brent had been watching her and realized that she had no clue where anything was in the kitchen. "The plates are in the cabinet above the sink to the right and the glassed are to the right. You'll find silver wear in the draw to the right of the sink."

She smiled at him. "Thanks." He just shrugged his shoulders like it was no big deal.

Anna walked back to the table with a cinnamon roll and a cup of coffee."

Brent stood from the table and pushed his chair in. "I'm going to go and start working. I'll see you two later."

Anna thought that it was odd that right after she had sat down Brent had left. Hmm, he invited her here, yet he doesn't want to spend time with her, how peculiar.

Something on Anna's face must have given away what she was thinking because Cassie spoke up. "Don't worry he's not that comfortable around females he's not related to, just give him some time, I'm sure he'll warm up to you."

"You're probably right." Anna looked around and then back at Cassie. "I was wondering if you could show me around the ranch. I'd really like to get to know this place."

As soon as Anna said that Cassie's eyes lit up. "I was hoping you would ask me to show you around." She looked at Anna who was still eating and spoke again. "We can go once you're finished eating."

Quickly Anna ate the rest of her cinnamon roll and then washed it down with the last of her coffee. She put her dishes in the dishwasher and then followed Cassie outside.

It took Anna a few seconds for her eyes to readjust too the brightness of the sun. The ranch was just as beautiful during the day as it was the night. As she was looking around she noticed things that she hadn't seen the night before. About two hundred yards away from the house, to the right there was a huge barn that must hold at least twenty or more horses. Across from the barn there were multiple corrals, all ranging in size.

The ranch was huge, it was over seven acres and she knew it to be true because as far as she could she it was rolling hills and mountains. No other buildings really except for the four nice bunkhouses to the right of the barn.

Anna looked over at the barn and saw all the horses eating their breakfasts of oats. Growing up on her parent's farm she'd loved going out and spending time with the horses.

"Hey, Cassie can we go over and see the horses?" Anna wanted go and meet them so bad, that she was shaking with anticipation.

"Of course, but I'm going to warn you know." Cassie said as they began their walk over to the barn."

"Warn me about what?" Anna was confused, why would Cassie need to warn her about something.

Cassie looked back over at Anna. "Well, Brent's horse, Maverick is not very friendly and he has a temper, he dislikes everyone that's not Brent."

Anna thought that Cassie comment was comical. "So he's just like your brother." She let out a laugh. "No wonder why they get along so well."

Cassie bumped Anna's shoulder playfully. "Come on he's not that bad. Just wait and he'll warm up to you."

When they entered the barn Cassie directed Anna over to her horse. He was a light brown American quarter horse. "This is my baby, Murphy."

Anna was loving being in the barn. She rubbed Murphy on the nose, he leaned his head into Anna's touch. She smiled at Murphy. "You're a sweet boy aren't you?"

He neighed loudly when Cassie began to give him a good rub. "He is, anytime you pet him or give him a good rub he's your best friend." Once again Murphy neighed and nodded his head as if he agreed with Cassie. "You'll also find that most of the horses on the ranch are either American paints or American quarter horses."

Anna smiled at Cassie. "That's great; my favorite breed is the quarter horse."

They continued meeting with the horses. When they came to the last horse Anna took one look at him and it was like love at first sight. He too was a quarter horse like Murphy but he was a dark brown almost black color. "Oh, Cassie what's his name?"

"This is Cupid. He currently isn't paired up with one of the hands."

Anna held out an apple for Cupid that she'd gotten from the pale beside his stall, and then she fed it to him. "You like that boy don't you?" Cupid nodded his head. Anna looked over at Cassie. "Can I ride him? Please." She begged.

"Of course, it seems like he likes you."

She'd only known cupid for a few minutes, but she already loved him. "I'm glad because I like him too."

Cassie looked at Anna before she began to leave the barn. "You two can hang out in here and get to know each other." She pointed to the corral outside the barn where the hands were milling around. "I'm just going to go see if the hands need anything. I'll see you later."

Anna nodded and then turned back to Cupid.

While she was spending time with him she sniffed him and he smelled awful. So she took him over to the area in the barn that was designated for giving the horses baths. "Looks like its bath time Cupid."

*****

The hands were all chatting about the nerd when Cassie got to the corral she looked around, trying to locate a specific person. She glanced over to the far right of the group and spotted him.

Cassie almost started drooling when she saw all six feet of lean muscular male. Which meant only one thing, Clint was waiting for her. She walked over towards him and stealthily poked him in the side.

He yelped when he felt fingers poke him in the side. Turning around he saw Cassie. "Hey." He smiled.

"Hey, you." Cassie quickly looked around to see if she could see Brent around. He didn't approve of the hands being with his sister romantically, so she had to be extremely cautious. "So do you want to go and check the fenced with me?" She asked coyly and winked at him.

"You know I do, but what about your brother?" Clint asked nervously as he looked around, hoping no one was paying attention to them.

"Don't worry. Just meet me out at our tree in an half an hour. I'll have a lunched packed for us."

Clint nodded his head and went back to the corral to hang out with the guys. He really liked Cassie. She was only a couple years younger than him since he was twenty eight. God, he loved her smile and the way she looked at him could turn his legs to mush. He loved the feel of her brown hair in his fingers. The only problem was that he had nothing to offer her. That's why he worked on the ranch. He couldn't give her a home like she deserved.

God, how he wished he could give her everything.

*****

Brent walked into the barn at almost eleven. He was in a foul mood and he had no clue why. It had all started that morning when he saw Anna. She was so nice and he wanted like her, but he'd been hurt so bad a few years ago by the woman he was engaged to. She'd left a void in him and made it hard for him to trust other women.

Two years ago he'd dated Leslie and it'd gotten so serious that he'd proposed to her. Leslie told him yes and everything had been going fine until a week before their wedding.

He found her in a very compromising position with his best hand. He'd fired the hand on the spot, but Leslie well he'd broken of the engagement even though it broke his heart to let her go. She was his heart, his life, his everything.

In his head he knew that all women were not like Leslie, but he just couldn't convince his heart that it was true.

After Brent entered the barn he saw Anna standing with Cupid. She looked beautiful with her hair falling in her face as she worked diligently on saddling Cupid. He felt a pull towards her, almost like he was attracted to her.

No!!! He couldn't be thinking like that. If he opened up to her, and let his guard down, then that would make him vulnerable. He just couldn't open his heart up and take the risk of being hurt again.

Brent crossed over to Anna. "What are you doing?" He snapped.

The look on Anna's face was of pure shock. "I'm just saddling up Cupid here." She smiled at him hoping that it would help take the edge off of his anger. "I thought I'd help him get some exercise."

That smile... No he couldn't think about that. "Who told you could ride him?" His anger was still as venomous as it had been before, so much for hoping one of her famous smiles would work.

Anna was starting to get pissed. He needed to grow up and put on his big boy pants. "Cassie told me I could." She said kindly. Why not kill him with a little kindness, while she was at it.

"You can ride." He laughed harshly.

'Wow, what an ass', she thought. "Yes, I can ride." She was full on pissed now. "Why don't you go back to whatever you were doing and leave me alone."

Brent turned to walk away. No women had ever called him out. "Oh, while you're at it..." he turned back around. "Why don't you grow up and put on your big boy pants." Brent walked away feeling like he'd been put in his place and then some.

Anna walked out of the barn with cupid. She needed a good long hard ride to get that man out of her head. Damn him, damn him, damn him. Why was he being such an ass?

Anna mounted Cupid and took off. She needed time and space to cool off from her run in with Brent.

Chapter 5

Chapter 5

Anna had been riding around for a couple hours when she realized that she had no clue where she was, and she had no idea how to get back to the barn.

Stupid Brent, this was all his fault. If he hadn't been so cruel and rude in the barn then she wouldn't be lost in a place that was foreign to her. Anna rode cupid over the ridge and spotted a very big whitebark pine tree. The tree was the perfect place for Anna to wait until help came.

Quickly she looked at her phone trying to see if she could get service, but it was no use there were no bars on her smartphone. Anna couldn't help but think that smartphones are just dumb phones in disguise.

After Anna had dismounted Cupid she tied his reins to the tree, and grabbed a book out of her saddlebags. The book was a romance novel. Anna had a soft spot for them. She could get lost in one so quickly, and then only emerge for reading it once she'd finished it. It was her guilty pleasure.

When Anna was reading romance novels she could just let go and relax, just being herself. Anna loved to read romance novels because they were her escape, but more than that they helped her believe that she could really find love and have it last forever. One of the reasons she was in Montana was because she'd decided to try and take a chance on love, but that was only a small reason why she was in Montana.

Cupid neighed in protest when Anna sat down and began to read. Anna just tried to ignore him. It was easier than admitting defeat to a horse.

The cover of the book was of a shirtless cowboy, much to her delight. She began reading about a brooding man and his trouble with falling in love, and the sweet girl that came along and helped heal his heart so that he could love her, like she did him.

*****

If there was one thing Brent felt, it was guilty. He hadn't seen Anna since he yelled at her, and that had been hours ago. It was now approaching five o'clock and he was starting to get antsy about not being able to find Anna anywhere.

He'd asked the hands if they'd seen Anna, but half of them had no clue who he was talking about and the other half had no clue where she was or where she could be.

Although he had found out that Clint and Cassie were checking the fences, and should be back soon, which was odd because none of the fences where damaged, well at least not that he knew of.

Maybe he should just go and look around again. He hadn't checked to see if she was in her room. He'd just go there first and if she wasn't there then he'd check everywhere else again, maybe he'd ride out and see if she'd gone for a ride.

Brent walked over to the house and when he arrived at her room he knocked hesitantly, but no one answered. Maybe she was asleep, so he knocked again but louder and longer this time. Still there was no answer. Okay, so she wasn't in her room. He looked around the rest of the house, and he still couldn't find her. Brent was really nervous and it didn't help that he felt guilty.

Back outside he looked anywhere there was a place she could be and yet he still couldn't find her. Brent walked over to the barn so that he could get Maverick saddled to ride out and look for her. As he was walked to the tack room he saw that Cupid's stall was empty, and then it all came back to him.

That's right when he'd made an ass out of himself she'd been getting Cupid saddled for a ride. So she was out in the range.

As fast as Brent could he grabbed his stuff from the tack room, and then walked to maverick's stall to saddle him.

Maverick's eyes lit up when he saw Brent - the only person his eyes lit up for - Brent quickly brushed down Mav's back. "Hey, boy we're going to go for a ride and see Anna."

Mav neighed loudly in agreement. Wow, the horse liked Anna, he never liked anyone other than Brent. Maybe Anna wasn't so bad after all. If Mav liked her then that meant she was something special.

The only problem with that was that Mav had liked his previous ex-girl-friend, the one that had cheated on him with his best ranch hand. It wasn't enough that he'd found out she was cheating on him, but the fact that he'd found her in a compromising with the hand, had thrown him over the edge.

Quickly he finished saddling Maverick, and was leading him out of the barn when she spotted Cassie and Clint riding back on their horses. His first thought was, 'Good the fence is fixed.'

Cassie rode up to him and dismounted her horse, Murphy. "Hey, Brent, Where are you going?"

He shrugged his shoulders as he mounted Maverick. "I'm going to go find Anna. I said some things earlier that I regret and know I have no clue where she." He rode of once he was finished.

Cassie was dumb founded. In less than one day of getting to know her he'd made an as out of himself, and Cassie knew exactly whose fault it was.

That stupid bitch Leslie had to go and ruin love for Brent. Cassie had known she was trouble from the first time she'd met her, but she never would have thought she would cheat on him in front of everyone. The only one who hadn't known about it had been Brent but he'd found out a short time later. The irony of it all was that Cassie had warned him that Leslie was trouble and that's exactly what she'd turned out to be. Cassie was just glad Brent hadn't married the bitch.

Someday Cassie going to have to have a girls' day with Anna so that she could tell her all about Leslie, A.K.A. the bitch, which would ultimately explain why he distrusted love so much. Cassie wished she could give that bimbo a good talking to, she would do more but orange jumpsuits really didn't suit her.

She looked over at Clint with a grim expression on her face. "We've got to help him. Leslie did a number on him."

Clint nodded as he dismounted. Together they hand in hand - since Brent wasn't around - walked to the barn to take care of their horses.

*****

Anna's reading was interrupted when she heard the sounds of a horse and a rider of in the distance. She quickly finished the page she was on and bookmarked it.

Looking up Anna realized that the rider was male but not much more because he was still a good distance away. She hoped and prayed that it wouldn't be Brent, she didn't know if she'd be able to help another argument from occurring between them.

As the rider got closer Anna groaned on the inside. She should stop wishing for things because obviously her fairy godmother was not up to granting them, especially when it came to Brent.

When Brent was ten feet away from Anna she stood up and put her book up, she then untied Cupids reins from the tree. Brent dismounted Maverick and then Anna spoke. "I'm glad you found me. I kind of got lost," she said as she motioned around with her arms.

There was a scowl on Brent's face when she looked up at him. He spoke. "Don't you know how dangerous it is to go out riding in a place you don't know how to navigate?"

'Great the Brent from this morning is back,' was the first thing Anna thought when he spoke.

"I do Brent, but I needed to vent, and I think you know why." He nodded remembering how he'd acted. "So you understand. Now if you'd kindly give me directions back to the ranch, it would be greatly appreciated."

He took his Stetson off his head and scratched the back of his head. "I think that you should come with me back to the ranch, instead of me giving you directions, and running the risk of you getting lost again."

What did he think she was, stupid? Well she wasn't. She knew she should have asked for directions and now he was trying to scold her for not doing so. That was pissing her off to no end.

"If I would have had directions I wouldn't have gotten lost..." She paused. "Which I take full blame for not asking for, but if you do give me directions know, I won't get lost getting back to the ranch."

Brent seemed to consider it for a few seconds. "No."

Great he was pissing her off for the second time that day. "Why, no?" She asked with restrained anger.

"I would just feel better if I could guide you back."

Guide her, she didn't need his guidance. "I don't need you guidance back to the ranch." Her tone was extremely harsh.

"I don't care if you don't need it. I was worried earlier when you were gone and I couldn't find you." His tone was rising now. "Do you know how dangerous it is out here?" He waited for her to response but there wasn't one. "There are mountain lions in this state. You could have been attacked by one. And then where would that leave you. That's right you would be dead most likely."

Anna was speechless. Completely and utterly speechless, she'd just been scolded. She felt awful and that just made her angrier. "I'm sorry, okay. I didn't mean to be so careless. Please just please give me the directions." She pleaded. "I just don't want to be with you, or ride with you for that matter," she snapped at him.

Great he'd made an ass out for a second time today, he realized. Maybe he should just give her the directions and let her ride of by herself, and then later he would try and apologize for being such an ass to her. If he was even capable of apologizing to a person, currently he was only capable of being an ass when it came to Anna.

When Anna looked over at Brent he looked like he was lost in his thoughts. She didn't need him to be thinking, she just needed directions. "So, about those directions..." She trailed off with a hint of anger.

"Go north..." He said pointing north. "About two miles and then go west another three miles and you should see the barn off in the distance. Got it?"

Anna mounted Cupid. "Yeah I got it."

Brent watched Anna riding off hoping that he'd given her enough distance so that she'd cool off and then let him apologize. Something inside of him felt off but he didn't know why...

*****

I hope you liked this chapter! I think I'm going to add this story to the 2013 Watty Awards! It would be great if you guys could keep commenting, voting, and reading!!!

How did you like Brent's ditsy moments in this Chapter? Don't worry he will redeem himself when it comes to Anna soon. The picture on the side is of Cupid. The song on the side doesn't really have anything to do with this chapter, but I think it fits Anna pretty well, she only knows how to be country and not really anything else. Thanks for reading!!!

Chapter 6

Chapter 6

Walking into her room later that night, Anna realized that she needed to talk to someone. Not Cassie she didn't want to talk to someone who was probably going to stand up for Brent. And talking to Brent that was out of the question, she'd probably yell at him, and then they'd end up in another fight, and Anna didn't want to fight anymore. The only person that left was Chrissie.

Oh, how she missed her best friend. It'd been a little over a day since she'd seen her and Anna missed Chrissie like crazy. Anna grabbed the house phone off of her nightstand and then dialed her friend's phone number. The phone rang a couple of times before Chrissie finally answered.

Chrissie's voice came on the other end of the line. "Who is this?" Chrissie asked.

That's right Chrissie didn't know this phone number because it was Brent's house phone. "It's me Anna, Chrissie."

The next time Chrissie spoke her voice sounded happy. "How is Montana? Tell me everything especially if it's about this Brent guy."

"I already love Montana. It reminds me of home when my parent's accepted me in their family. Cassie, Brent's little sister is like the little sister I never had." Anna paused not knowing if she should tell Chrissie about Brent and their arguments. "And Brent well, he's a little distant and grumpy, but I'm sure we'll get along someday."

Chrissie was confused from what Anna had told her in New York this guy was great, but know she was saying that he was distant and grumpy. "What do you mean you'll get along someday? Anna from what you told me in New York this guy is supposed to be great, amazing but now you're telling that he's distant and grumpy. What's going on there?"

"I don't know we tend to butt heads a lot but I think that was we get to know each other a little better we'll start to get along," she paused. "Chrissie he is a great guy even though he's grumpy and distant. Everything here is great except for the fact that..."

"That what?" Chrissie said insistently.

Anna paused preparing to speak. "We fought... well not really fought, it was more like we kept finding reasons to yell at each other."

Anna knew what was coming. Back in New York Chrissie told her that if this Brent guy was an ass then she was coming back to New York and they'd find another way for her to get out of the city.

Chrissie sounded Angry not at Anna, but at Brent. "Anna I want you to come back to New York and now. What if this guy hurts you?"

Anna loved Chrissie but sometimes she could be bossy. "Chrissie he's not that kind of a guy and I'm not coming back to New York unless it's for a visit."

"But Anna as you said you don't know him, so you can't possibly know what kind of guy he is."

Anna was sitting on the bed nut she shifted and moved around so that she could get more comfortable. This conversation wasn't going the way she thought that it would. "Chrissie I know enough about Brent to know that he would never hurt me."

"Fine, but if you guys keep fighting I'm going to personally fly to Montana and bring you back with me. Okay?" Chrissie sounded a little defeated.

"Okay."

"What's the country like I've never really been to a place that wasn't a big or small city?" Chrissie asked curiously."

Anna let out a deep breath. "Chrissie it's beautiful, so calm and quiet. I took a ride to day on one of the horses, Cupid and it the land was covered in hills and trees. People talk about the Montana sky, but they do not do it justice. It's not beautiful it's breathtaking, gorgeous..." She paused getting a little emotional. "It reminds me of home all of the open land that no one has had a chance to turn into a busy city."

"Wow Anna it sounds amazing and beautiful just like you said. I am most definitely going to have to come for a visit and get myself a cowboy." Chrissie said jokingly about the cowboy part.

That was why she loved Chrissie; she could turn anything into a joking matter. "Maybe you should come and visit. The cowboys her are some of the finest you will ever find." She said seriously with a hint of amusement.

Just then there was a knock on Anna's door. "Hey, Chrissie I'm going to have to call you back later there's someone at my door waiting to talk to me."

Chrissie sounded a little bummed when she spoke. "Okay just call back so that we can continue our conversation."

"Of course I will."

"Bye, girly."

"Bye, Chrissie." Anna quickly ended the phone call and began to walk to the door after she'd got off the bed. She turned the nob praying that it wasn't Brent on the other side.

*****

Brent got back to the barn shortly after Anna had taken care of Cupid. Quickly Brent put Maverick up in the barn and then he went back to the house.

Cassie was waiting for him when he entered the house. "Big brother what exactly did you do to her?" She got no response. "She is locked in her room talking to someone on the phone. I swear if she's making plans to leave then I am going to be pissed. She is one of the best things that has ever happened to you."

"How is she the best thing that has ever happened to me?" Brent asked.

"She is stubborn enough to handle your grumpy backside, sweet enough to be able to love you, and do so for the rest of your life. Plus there is an attraction between the two of you I can see it and I know that you know it's there." Cassie paused. "Now go apologize for being an ass today."

"You don't need to tell me what do Cassie. I was already planning on saying sorry I just wanted to make sure she'd cooled off some first." With that he walked out of the living room and to the staircase.

Brent stood in front of the door to Anna's room. He could hear her talking to someone on the phone talking about Montana. She was saying how it was such a beautiful place and how what people say about the Montana sky doesn't do it justice.

Pride shot through him. She loved his home and his land. Maybe Cassie was right about her. Maybe she was the best thing that could have ever happened to him. Hearing her saying all that stuff gave him the courage to knock on her door. At first he hesitated for a couple of seconds but then he knocked.

He could hear her saying goodbye to whoever she was talking to. Then he heard the faint noise of sheets rustling as if she was getting of her bed and then he heard her walking towards the door.

The door knob twisted slightly at first and then all the way. The door opened and Anna was standing there. She looked beautiful to Brent. The light in her room cast a glow around her, making her look like an angel standing before him.

"I just wanted to say that I'm sorry for the way I acted earlier." He said nervously as he shuffled his feet.

Anna looked like she was mildly surprised by his apology. "I accept your apology and I have one too give you."

"You don't have to do that."

"Oh, but I do. The arguments weren't completely your fault. I admit at times my temper can be a little short. So I am sorry for the way I acted earlier as well."

Things between them became tense for a moment while the attraction between them sparked and fizzled. Brent couldn't help it anymore he moved closer to her and put his hands on her waist and then he pulled her even closer. His voice was husky when he spoke. "Apology accepted."

Anna couldn't move just stare into his eyes. She was frozen in place. There was a part of her that wanted him to bridge the distance between their mouths and kiss her senseless. The other part told her that she couldn't his moods swung too much. One minute hot the next cold.

She was stunned when Brent lowered his mouth to hers. His mouth slanted over hers lightly at first. Anna opened her mouth as if she was going to protest but then she stuck her tongue out to meet his halfway. Then it became more urgent and hungry. By the time Anna pulled away they were both out of breath. It was the best kiss either of them had ever had.

Anna pulled out of Brent's grasp. "Wh-what was that about?" She didn't even wait for a response from him. She was so stunned that she turned around and locked herself in her room. Anna leaned against her door and pressed her fingers to her mouth. One word escaped them, "Wow!"

Not once in her life had Anna ever been kissed like that. It had felt so perfect, she'd never felt like that after a kiss. There was one thing Anna knew and she knew that she was more attracted to Brent then she had ever been to another person in her whole life.

That night both Anna and Brent laid awake not able to think about anything other than the amazing kiss they'd shared. In the morning they'd have to face each other and talk about the attraction they shared. But for that one night they could just think about that one kiss and nothing more.

*****

So that kiss...

I know this chapter is short but I hope you like it. I think the song on the side is fitting for this chapter, Are You Gonna Kiss Me Or Not by Thompson Square. I hope you enjoyed this chapter!!! Please comment and vote if you did!

Chapter 7

Chapter 7

Sleeping had been virtually impossible. Brent had never lost a full night of sleep, not even when he'd broken off his engagement with Leslie, but that one kiss had kept running through his head all night making him unable to sleep.

At six in the morning Brent drug his butt out of bed. With a loud yawn he walked to his master bathroom door. After he entered his bathroom he stripped down to his birthday suit. The hot water felt amazing as it pelted his body, relieving his tense muscles. Brent reluctantly stepped out of the shower when the water began to become cold.

Wrapping a towel around his waist he quickly shaved and brushed his teeth. Brent exited his bathroom and crossed to his closet. He grabbed a pair of jeans and a plaid shirt to put on.

After putting his boots on and grabbing his phone he exited his room to go down stairs for breakfast. The one thing that kept running through his head the whole time he was getting ready was that one mind blowing, earth shattering kiss. Brent knew one thing, he had to find a way to repeat that kiss, but first he had to see if Anna was willing to be with him.

*****

Anna was applying her makeup after he'd showered and dressed. She kept putting cover up on the bags under her eyes. After applying it twice and still seeing the purple she said, to hell with it. There was no use in trying to hide the fact that she hadn't gotten one minute of sleep, it was plain to see in the slow, sluggish movements she was making.

She exited her room and turned to go down the stairs. It was a quarter before seven in the morning, so Cassie and Brent should be down stairs eating breakfast at the moment.

Cassie was sitting at the small breakfast table when Anna entered the kitchen. There was cereal, milk, orange juice, and some fresh fruit sitting on the table.

"I didn't feel like cooking or baking this morning so that's why we have cereal and fruit for breakfast." Cassie said as she took a sip of her coffee.

"Cassie you know that if you ever need help around here just ask. I'd be more than happy to help," she paused. "Actually I should already be helping you around the house."

"That would be great. I've missed having another female around to help out around here. I've been having to do it all since mom and dad retired to Wyoming."

Anna sad down next to Cassie and grabbed a bowl. "How are they? I can't wait to meet them."

Cassie passed Anna the cereal and milk. "They're doing well. I haven't heard form then in almost a week."

"That's great. When do you think I'll be able to meet them?"

Cassie messed with her coffee cup, spinning it around on the table slowly, so that she wouldn't spill any of her coffee. "Soon hopefully. Since its mid-October you should meet them in a little over a month when they come to visit for thanks giving." Cassie smiled at Anna. "You'll love mom, she's the sweetest person you'll ever meet, and dad well he's a lot like Brent, they tend to butt heads a lot."

Anna poured some milk over her cereal. "They sound like really great people."

As Anna took her first bite of cereal Brent walked into the kitchen. The mood of the room instantly became tense and awkward.

"Hey, Brent." Cassie said.

"Hey sis, what's for breakfast?" Brent asked.

"Cereal, juice, and some fresh fruit." She said gesturing to the food on the table in front of her.

"Looks great." He said barely acknowledging Anna's existence.

Brent sat down across from Anna so that she had no choice but to look at him.

Cassie began to speak. "So are you two an item now or something?"

Both Anna and Brent immediately tensed up. "Why do you ask?" Brent asked Cassie.

"Oh, just because I heard you guys kissing last night and neither of you came down for dinner," she said with a grin on her face.

Now it was Anna's turn to speak. "Honestly Cassie we haven't talked about are relationship status." She paused. "And as for the kiss, how'd you know about it?"

Cassie through her fist up in the air triumphantly. "So you two did kiss. I want all the details." Brent grunted as he took a bite of cereal.

"Seriously Cassie, can't you mind your own business. This needs to be taken care of between Anna and me." He said.

Cassie sighed defeated. "Oh, fine I'll leave you two alone to talk." She got up from the table taking her coffee cup with her. She set it in the sink and then left the house to look for one cowboy in peculiar, Clint.

Brent kept eating his cereal and looking at the paper next to him after Cassie left the two of them alone.

"Brent what's going on between us?" Anna asked seriously looking him straight in the eyes.

He looked up from his paper. "Frankly I know as much as you do about us, which is nothing."

Anna smiled shyly at Brent. "How about this..." She paused thinking over what she was about to say. "How about we just try to be friends right now and later on we can look into whatever there is between us."

Brent looked like he was thinking over what she'd just said. "Sure why not." He held out his hand to her. "Friends?"

She grabbed his hand from across the table and shook it. "Friends."

*****

Cassie walked out the front door looking around to see if she could spot her cowboy. Not seeing him around Cassie walked over to the barn. Clint was standing in front of the stall where his horse, Perseus was.

She snuck up behind him and out her hands in front of her eyes. "Guess who?" She asked in a sultry voice."

Clint played along. "Gee, I don't know, is it Carrie Underwood."

"Nope." She said popping the p. "Try again."

"Maybe it's Julianne Hough." He mused out loud.

She took her hands off of her eyes and pulled Clint to turn him around. She kissed him long and slow before she finally let him go. "You better have known it was me." She told him seriously.

Clint put his hands on her waist. "Of course I knew it was you."

"Good. Do you want to go into town with me today? We need some more supplies for around here and I could really use a big strong man to help get it." She said emphasizing his biceps.

"Sure just let me finish cleaning out the next couple of stalls and I'll be ready to go." He kissed her lightly on the lips and then he released her.

"Okay, I'll go and get my purse. Do you want to take my truck or yours?" she asked him.

Clint mulled the idea over in his head for a minute. "Let's take mine. I'll meet you out by the truck in a couple minutes."

Cassie left the barn for the house trying to remember where she had put her purse last.

She suddenly knew how she could help Brent and Anna. They could go into town and have a girl's day, go shopping and get manicures and pedicures. It had been so long since she'd gone into town and go shopping with another female around her own age. It was Tuesday now so they could go into town on Thursday or Friday.

Anna was wiping down the countertops in the kitchen when Cassie walked into the house. "Hey, Anna, I was wondering if you'd want to go into town with me on Thursday or Friday and have a girl's day with me." She paused, letting Anna mull the idea over. "We could go shopping, eat junk food, and get manicures and pedicures."

That idea sounded amazing to Anna. She could use a fun filled day to relieve some of the stress and tension she'd been feeling since she'd moved to Montana. "That sounds great. Either days fine with me."

"Great we can talk about it more tonight. I have to go into town to get some supplies, but I should be back for dinner."

"Sounds great. I can make dinner tonight. Just one question what's Brent's favorite thing to eat for dinner?" Anna asked with a sincere look on her face.

Cassie couldn't help but think, 'Ah, she's already starting to fall for him.'

"He loves beef stroganoff with French bread with butter -- which I can pick up while I'm in town. I would also make a salad to go with it." She said as she looked around for her person.

"Thanks I'll see you later. Have fun." Anna said as Cassie grabbed her purse and waved goodbye to her.

Cassie saw Clint standing by his truck when she exited the house the house. "You ready." He asked.

"Yeah, let's get going." She smiled up at him as she opened her door and climbed up into his truck.

They laughed and smiled their whole way into town.

Clint loved her, yet he felt bad about taking her up all her time when he could never marry her because he couldn't support her. He'd have to leave and make something of himself if he ever wanted to marry her. Which he did, more than anything else in this world.

*****

Here's the next chapter just like I promised. I hope you enjoy it! Please vote & comment!!!

The song on the side doesn't really have anything to do with this chapter, but it's kind of a prelude to what is going to happen between Cassie and Clint, he isn't going to die or be dead like the guy in the song. Enjoy!!!

Chapter 8

Chapter 8

"Something smells great." Brent said that night after he'd walked into the house.

Anna smiled shyly at him. "I made beef stroganoff with salad and French bread. Cassie said it was your favorite."

"It is Cassie hasn't made this in forever." He grabbed her wrist lightly and grinned at her. "Thanks."

Tingles shot up Anna's body and coursed through the rest of her body. "Cassie should be back any minute with the French bread and then we can eat."

Just as Anna finished speaking the front door closed. Both Brent and Anna left the kitchen to see who it was. Neither was shocked when they saw Cassie standing in the living room with a loaf of French bread in her hands.

Cassie walked over and handed Anna the loaf of bread. "Sorry guys I didn't think it would take that long to get all the supplies we needed from town."

It hadn't honestly taken that long but she didn't want them to know that she and Clint had gone to lunch and browsed the shops for a little while.

"No problem, we were just waiting for you to come home before we began eating." Anna said with an understanding look on her face. Anna had her suspicions on why it had taken Cassie so long in town. Brent had no clue of course that his baby sister was dating one of the ranch hands. She'd have to talk to Cassie about Clint when they were out on their little adventure in town.

Brent just stood in the living room watching Cassie and Anna chat. "Hey, little sis you might want to go wash up as well before we eat."

Cassie nodded and walked into the small bathroom located next to the office.

While they waited for Cassie to wash up Anna cut the bread. Brent helped by setting the bowls of food on the table.

When Cassie walked back into the little dining area in the kitchen they started to dish out the food.

"Wow, Anna this is great." Brent said as he smiled at her. Cassie nodded her head in agreement with her brother since her mouth was full.

A little bit of a blush formed on Anna's cheeks. "Thank you it's a family recipe that my grandmother passed down to me."

From then on the conversation revolved around everyone's days and how the ranch was doing. Once Brent mentioned Clint's name and Cassie face little up a little and her eyes softened as she thought about Clint.

Anna noticed the change in Cassie's expression, Brent just kept talking as if everything was normal, and his sister wasn't turning into a pile of mush beside him. Anna was most definitely going to have to talk to Cassie and get the scoop on her relationship with Clint.

Once dinner was finished Brent offered to help with the dishes but Cassie and Anna shooed him away. Cassie and Anna fell into a pattern, Anna washed while Cassie dried.

"While I was cooking I was thinking about our little outing and I remembered how the other day you said Fridays were the busiest days of the week around her so I thought we could have our girl's day on Thursday." Anna said in a quiet tone so that they wouldn't disturb Brent while he watched the football game on TV.

Cassie hadn't even thought about Friday being busy. "That sounds great I completely forgot about how busy Fridays are."

After washing all the dishes and putting them away. Anna and Cassie both said goodnight to Brent and retired to their rooms.

*****

The days before Cassie and Anna's girl's day passed by quickly and the morning of their outing they were up early so that they could finish the half our hour drive into town before eight. Most people when they saw walker, Montana on a map they figured that it was tiny town, but in reality it was quite large. The downs population was almost fifteen thousand. With that many people living there they were able to multiple schools of their own. Every morning school buses would go by the ranches that some of the children lived on and take them into town for school and then bring them home in the afternoons.

As the town came into view Cassie pointed out different areas where events were held or popular hangout places for the teens.

They had their own little branch of the Cattleman's Association since most of the land that surrounded Walker belonged to ranchers.

When they drove down Main Street it was filled with cute little shops and restaurants. Anna was surprised when she saw and old pharmacy that still had a functioning Soda Fountain inside of it. On the windows they advertised sundaes, egg creams, malts and even phosphate sodas.

Cassie smiled at Anna. "Cool huh. That soda fountain is still a popular hangout for teens. I used to go there after school and order and strawberry phosphate with all my friends."

"This town reminds me of the one I grew up near." Anna told Cassie.

"It's great you'll love it." Cassie said as she pulled into a parking lot and parked.

As Anna got out of the truck she inhaled. She loved the smell of Montana air it was so fresh and welcoming.

"There are a couple of shops I have to take you to and after we visit those we can look around and get some lunch." She paused letting everything she was saying sink in. "Then after lunch we have our manicure and pedicure appointments. I was thinking that before we go home we could stop by the Soda Fountain and get and get an ice cream or something."

Anna nodded. She was trying to take in the town she would be living near for the rest of her life.

Cassie grabbed Anna's hand and dragged her over to her favorite boutique, Country Girl Chic. The windows displayed fitted jeans with flannel but up shirts paired with a pair of to die for boots, but in the other window there were a couple of dresses. There was one that was just like a summer dress, but the other one Anna couldn't help but drool over it.

"I take it you like that dress," Cassie said.

"I do. It's beautiful." The dress looked like something a southern belle would wear. It was different shades of brown it had a lace bodice that ended at the belted waist. Then it cascaded down into ruffles the shades of brown getting darker the lower the ruffles went.

"Come on let's go try it on."

Anna nodded her head as she continued to stare at the dress.

Cassie opened the door and let Anna go ahead of her. There was a lady sitting at the register who looked to be a little older than Cassie but not as old as Anna. "Hey Lily, this is Anna. She wants to try that purple dress in the window.

Lily smiled at Anna. "Of course you two look around while I go get it."

"Cassie that wasn't necessary, I wouldn't be able to wear it till summer since it's so short." She said as she admired the dress some more.

"Just try it on, there's no harm in doing that. Is there?" Cassie asked.

"No I guess not and it is quite beautiful."

Anna went and looked around the boutique finding many things that she would love to have yet couldn't quite afford.

Lily approached Anna with the dress. "Here you go. I guessed on your size but I think it will fit you nicely."

Anna smiled at her. "Thanks." The turned to Cassie, "I'm going to go and try this on." Cassie just nodded her head and went back to looking through the racks of clothing. Her face had turned serious since Anna had last looked and her. She couldn't help but wonder why.

*****

The dress what perfect, it fit her perfectly in every single way it could. It also looked great with her boots. She normally would consider herself semi-pretty at her best but in that dress she looked beautiful.

Cassie was waiting for her when she exited the fitting room. "What do you think?" She asked as she admired herself in the mirror.

"You look beautiful. If my brother saw you in this dress he would be awestruck..." She paused knowing sometime today she was going to have to tell Anna about the bitch Leslie. "Speaking of my brother once you're out of that dress I have to tell you something about his past."

Anna couldn't tell if what Cassie was going to tell her was good or bad.

"Don't worry it's just something you should know." The look on Anna's face had been grim. "What did you think I was going to tell you that he was a serial killer or something?"

Anna's face turned white. "He's not I promise you." Cassie reassured her feeling bad for messing with her a little.

"That wasn't funny Cassie. You had me really worried." Anna told Cassie seriously.

Cassie held up her hands in surrender. "Okay, Okay I'm sorry." She said sheepishly.

Anna turned back to the dressing room to change. She was most definitely going to have to get Cassie back messing with her like that.

While Anna changed Cassie was thinking about the best way that she could tell Anna about Leslie and why her brother was so gun-shy with women.

Anna walked back out with the dress in her hands. "I'm going to purchase this dress real quick and then you can tell me whatever you want to tell me about Brent while we go to the other shops."

With Anna's bag in her hands she and Cassie made their way out of the boutique and into one of the other shops, except this was a shop that sold country home décor.

"So what is it that you want to tell me about Brent?" Anna asked curiously as she looked at some of the rigs they sold.

"He has a bad past with love."

*****

Thanks for reading! I know there's a cliff hanger, I'm sorry. This chapter was going to have everything about Leslie in it, but then I realized that it would have been too long. I hope you enjoyed it! Please vote and comment!

Chapter 9

Chapter 9

"Why? What happened to him?" Anna was genuinely curious and worried about what had happened to Brent.

Cassie sighed hating that she was going to have to tell someone about that depressing time in Brent's life. "A couple of years ago Brent started to date this girl named Leslie." Cassie paused not knowing how to best explain what had happened in the past.

"I thought she was really sweet and genuine when I first met her, not mention gorgeous and I mean gorgeous. She looked like a model right out of a country magazine. She was so sweet and kind, and when I looked at her she seemed like she really cared about him." Emotion was clogging Cassie's throat and she had to pause.

Anna came up to her and hugged her tight knowing this was hard for Cassie to talk about because she loved her brother so much. "It's okay Cassie you don't have to tell me if you don't want to."

"No, no I need to," Cassie said in a rush. "After they'd been dating a couple months Leslie started to ask subtle questions about the ranches finances and I told her not realizing what I was doing. I was like putty in her hands. By then my brother was so smitten with her - excuse my old fashion term - that he couldn't think straight anymore."

"One day she and Brent had gotten back from town and I had noticed that she was towing around bags with an assortment of items in them. Not to mention the new clothes she was wearing. He'd bought her a Stetson that must have cost him at least five-hundred dollars, and then the huge sterling silver belt buckle she was wearing - which I don't even want to know how much that cost him. Her boots were brand new as well, they were made of some expensive leather making them cost probably as much as her new Stetson had."

Cassie swallowed and willed her tears to stay at bay. "It all became so clear why she'd been asking about our finances and everything. She didn't really love him she was just trying to get as much as she could out of him. That enraged me so much."

"Oh, Cassie I'm so sorry that couldn't have been easy for you." Anna felt so bad for her; she'd been caught in the middle of a bad relationship because she'd known what Leslie had been up to.

"It wasn't." Cassie grabbed a knickknack from one of the shelves in the store and fidgeted with it. "I didn't know what to do, my brother was in love with her and she was using him. It took me a long time to tell him about what Leslie was doing, but he didn't believe me and told me not to lie to him."

"After they'd been dating for almost a year he proposed to her and she'd accepted. For a while he wasn't buying her as much stuff and I couldn't help but think that maybe it had been a phase in their relationship that was over."

Cassie felt like crying as she continued on. "Then a couple weeks before their wedding I caught her out in the stable with one of the hands. Let's just say they were in a very compromising position on one of the hay bales. I was shocked I never thought that she would cheat on my brother."

"Wow she really was a bitch." Anna had spoken the words in her head before she could stop them. "Sorry, go on."

"You don't have to be sorry she really was a bitch." Cassie had a little bit of a smile gracing her face after what Anna had said. "Anyways the next day I confronted her and told her about how I knew about her wild nights with one of our hands. At first she claimed that they weren't true and the she told me that if I ever told Brent she'd make sure he got rid of me."

Cassie couldn't hold the tears at bay anymore. "I believed her even though I knew Brent would never have done something like that to me." Cassie let out a sob. "I should have told him. The whole town knew and he hadn't figured it out yet.

"Then about a week before the wedding Leslie made another trip out to the barn except this one was during the day. All the hands had the day off and she thought that Brent was going to be in town for the day."

Cassie paused before she told Anna the rest of what had happened. "She was having another rendezvous with the same hand. Brent had finished his business in town early and when he came home he went to the barn to put everything up except he'd found her - much like I had - with the hand in the barn on a hay bale in that same compromising position. I'd never seen him angrier he left the barn and went into their room. He took all of her stuff and through it out onto the front lawn."

"By then Leslie had realized that Brent had caught her. She tried to tell him that it was the hand and he'd been trying to rape her, but he hadn't bought it for one second. That was where I came in. I told him that she was lying and not to believe a word I said. That just enraged Leslie more. She tried to slap me but Brent had grab her hand told her that if she even thought about it he'd be calling the cops and have her hauled off to jail." Anna couldn't help but be awestruck by what Cassie was telling her.

"She threw her ring at him after that and left with all of her stuff. Brent was so angry. He fired the ranch hand that he'd caught her with and then after that he'd gone back into the house and he drank himself into a stupor."

"Wow." Was all Anna could say, she felt so bad for Brent and the way he'd been treated by the woman he'd loved. Who could be that conniving and evil?

Cassie whipped at the tears on her face. She gave Anna a sad smile. "I just wanted you to know why my brother shies away from love. I think that if anyone can help him heal his heart and help him to love again, it's you."

Anna was reeling from what Cassie had just said. "Thanks, I think."

"You're welcome."

They continued looking through the store, but Cassie's confession about Brent's past love life had created a little bit of an uncomfortable tension between the two of them.

Both Cassie and Anna found pieces of décor that they couldn't live without. "I think I can make my room a little homier with some of the stuff I bought," Anna said as they exited the store and began walking down the street.

"It doesn't feel like home?" Cassie questioned Anna.

"It does. It's just that I'm still adjusting and some of my stuff hasn't arrived yet so I can't really decorate the way I want to and make it feel like home.

"Oh." They passed by a little café and Cassie pulled Anna with her. "Let's go in here and get some lunch before we go to our appointments at the nail salon." Annie agreed.

When they walked in the café they were led to a table, and told that their server would be coming by soon to take there order. Both of them were starving from all the shopping they'd done.

Cassie's nose was still buried in the menu looking at her meal options when Anna spoke. "Cassie is it okay if I ask you something and you not get mad or offended?"

Cassie looked up from her menu and spoke slowly as if she was unsure of here answer. "Sure."

"I've seen you and Clint together and I was just curious as to what's going on between the two of you." Anna knew what was going on with them, but she wanted Cassie to tell her herself and confirm what she already knew to be true.

"If I tell you, you have to promise me not to tell Brent." She held her pinky up to Anna. "Pinky swear?"

Anna grasped Cassie's pinky with her own. "I swear. Now tell me."

Just then the waitress came and Cassie took a calming breath knowing that she could hold off telling Anna the truth for a minute.

The waitress was in her early thirties and she was wearing an apron that said, Jane's Café, "My name is Jane and I will be your server. What can I get the two of you?"

Anna figured that Jane was probably the owner of the café. "Can I get a glass of iced tea and your BLT on wheat with fries?"

"Sure thing," the waitress said and then turned to Cassie for her order. "What about for you?"

Cassie glanced at her menu one last time and then she began to speak. "I would also like a glass of iced tea and a Caesar salad with the breast of chicken."

The waitress, Jane nodded her head yes. "Okay, I've got two iced teas, one BLT on wheat with fries and a Caesar salad with the breast of chicken."

Both Cassie and Anna nodded yes, and Jane left to go place their order.

"Okay, now you have to tell me Cassie," Anna said once the waitress was gone.

"I don't know where to start." Cassie said as she blew out a breath of air.

"How about starting at the beginning." Anna suggested.

"Yeah sure I think I can do that. About a year ago Brent was looking and Clint showed up. At first look I didn't think anything of him; he was just another ranch hand." Cassie had a dreamy look in her eyes as she continued. "Then one day Brent sent us to check on the fences and while we were riding, Murphy got spooked by a snake and he threw me."

"Were you okay?"

"Yeah I was fine. After I fell I just laid there not ready to move yet. Clint kneeled down next to me and gathered me up in his arms. It had felt like something electric had shot through me and when I looked at Clint's eyes and I could tell he'd felt it too, but more than that he'd been so gentle with me that it'd melted my heart a little."

"So what'd you guys do?" Anna asked.

"We didn't do anything. You see this happened after Brent dumped Leslie and he made an official rule that no hands were allowed to date me. Before it had been applied, but now it was official and I could tell that Clint wasn't willing to lose his job over me."

"I'm sorry Cassie."

"Why? We're together now and that's all that matters." The waitress brought by their teas and Cassie took a sip of hers.

"Well I know that, but at that time you couldn't be together." Anna said as she laid her napkin across her lap.

"Yeah, it bummed me out for a while. Clint and I worked so well together, and so Brent would always pair us up to do work which I'm not gonna lie it was hell." She smiled to herself thinking about Clint. "Then one day I couldn't take it anymore. We were by ourselves fixing fences and I dropped my hammer, and thought, 'What the hell.' So I kissed him we were both shocked afterwards and just held each other in a hug. After that we decided we both needed to be together no matter the consequences and that's the way it's been ever since."

"I'm so happy for you. From what I've seen of Clint he's a great guy. I think he'll make you very happy."

"Ah, thanks Anna. I think he'll make me very happy, too."

Anna sat there for a moment considering her next question. "Cassie, do you think you guys will ever get married?

Cassie was slightly stunned by Anna's question. She fiddled with the straw in her ice tea. "I hope so, why do you ask?" Cassie took a sip of tea trying to keep herself busy.

"I don't know, it's just I've been here for a little while now and I've gotten to know you, and I already consider you to be like a sister. I just want you to be happy."

Brent had picked well - of course with Cassie's guidance - Anna was such a sweet and caring person. The exact kind of person Cassie would pick for her brother. "I am and I love Clint so much. He's been a little different lately, and I think that he might ask me to marry him soon."

"That's great news. I promise you that if Brent flips out about it I'll be on your side and try to help." That was such great news for Cassie, Clint would be a wonderful husband to her.

Shortly later the waitress dropped off their food. They both dug in, hungry from their shopping trip.

Once they'd finished eating they paid their tab and walked down the street to the nail salon. They were greeted by a teenage girl at the reception desk who led them over to the chairs where their pedicures were to be done.

While they got their nails done they talked about girl stuff, and every once in a while the conversation would be about Clint and Brent, but for the most part Anna hadn't minded talking about Brent in a romantic way. She could honestly see herself married to him in the future.

*****

I'm sorry it took me so long to get this chapter up. I'm going to apologize in advance. These next couple of months are going to be extremely busy for me, and I just want you all to know that I might not be posting chapters as frequently as I have been. I'll try to get chapters up when I can, but as I said I'm going to be extremely busy.

The song on the side is Somebody's Heartbreak by Hunter Hayes. I feel like this song is a little fitting for this story at times.

Thanks for reading!!! I hope you enjoyed this chapter!!! Please vote and comment!!!

Chapter 10

Chapter 10

That night after Cassie and Anna had gone to bed, Brent sat out on the front porch in one of the rocking chairs. He thought about his parents, who were currently retired in Wyoming, but he remembered when they'd sit outside at night taking about anything and everything. Brent missed them which was the reason why he was sitting outside staring at the moon thinking about everything.

Since his kiss with Anna, he couldn't sleep at night because every time he closed his eyes he would remember how she felt wrapped up in his arms, and that kiss, well it kept repeating itself making him think that he might go crazy if he didn't repeat it, and soon. He cursed himself for deciding to be just friends with her right now. He wanted to be more than that with her. He wasn't sure what more entitled yet, but he still wanted it.

When he'd lay awake he'd wonder if Anna was staring at her ceiling like he was with his, thinking about him and that kiss.

Maybe he could ask her on a date. Saturday there was supposed to be a local country artist playing at the Broken String Tavern in town and there was sure to be some dancing. He could hold her close and feel her body pressed flesh up against his while they danced. The thought was quickly becoming an intoxicating one for Brent.

A date with Anna was just what he needed. He'd be able to get to know her better which would make him happy and then maybe they could start acting like a couple since that's what everyone thought them to be.

The sound of a person walking towards Brent brought him back from his thoughts. When he looked up he couldn't quite tell who it was at first and then as the figure started to get closer he realized it was Clint. Brent wondered why Clint would be coming to talk to him this late at night. Something must be wrong with the hand, but what was it?

He'd have pry to get the answer out of him somehow.

As Clint stood on the porch the look on his face was a grave one. The look was unusual on his normally emotionless face.

Clint to took off his Stetson off and held it against his thigh. "Hey, Brent can I talk to you for a minute?"

"Sure what's up?" He motion towards him to sit in the rocking chair next to him."

As Clint down he sighed sadly. "I don't really know how to say this."

"Say what?" Brent asked curiously.

Once again Clint sighed, and then he took a deep breath. "I think that my time at the ranch has come to an end. I know that this is short notice, but I'd like to leave your employment on Sunday morning."

Brent was stunned by what Clint had just said. He wondered why Clint was leaving with such short notice. "I guess that'd be fine, but can I ask you why you're leaving?"

Because I love your sister and as long as I'm here I can never provide for her what she'll need, he thought. "I don't know, I just feel like it's time to move on." Something inside of Clint screamed liar.

"Okay, I'll have your last paycheck for you Saturday afternoon." Brent rubbed his face with the palm of his hand. "It's going to be different around here without you Clint. You were one of my best hands."

Clint looked up at the Montana sky and knew immediately that he'd miss it, but more than that he'd miss Cassie. "Brent I have one more favor to ask of you."

"Sure what is it?" He asked. Clint was just full of surprises tonight.

"I'd like to tell everyone when I want to that I'm leaving, and not have it spread around the ranch first thing in the morning." He needed to be the one to tell Cassie. Having her find out from someone else would not be good for his health or his heart, as it was leaving her was going to be hard enough for him.

Brent thought that that was an odd favor to ask for, but he kept his thoughts to himself. Clint's business was none of Brent's concern, that was unless it was hurting someone he cared for, and he didn't think that it would.

"Do whatever you need." Brent told Clint and then they both stood up from the rocking chairs. Brent held his hand out Clint and he shook it. "It's been good having you around. If you ever need a job, just come back and one will be waiting for you."

Clint let go of Brent's hand and nodded. "Thanks I'll do that if the need ever arises."

*****

He was going to leave his love. The honorable Clint was going to leave the only woman he'd ever loved. Breaking Cassie's heart was going to end up breaking his own and bring him immense heartache like he'd never known. The only problem was that he had to do it.

Clint had nothing to offer her. Okay, so that wasn't true, he had his heart, but that was all. His love wasn't enough. He needed to know that he could take care of her financially, and currently he couldn't or at least not as much as he wanted to.

He wanted to be his own man. Clint wanted to own and run his own ranch so that he could provide for Cassie. Don't get him wrong, Clint had liked working for Brent. Being a ranch hand just wasn't a stable enough lifestyle for him to have a wife and raise children in, and oh how he wanted to see Cassie's stomach grow round with his children.

Clint was going to leave her.

He wouldn't be gone too long - hopefully - just long enough for him to save up enough money for him to start his own ranch.

Then, well then he'd come back and propose to Cassie that is if she'd still have him. Knowing Cassie though, she'd make him work for it, but he would. Cassie would be his wife, the mother of his children, someday.

Now, he just had to figure out when to tell her. Hopefully when he did she wouldn't castrate him, he liked his masculine parts to much for that. She wouldn't though, or at least Clint didn't think that she would. Cassie loved him far too much to do anything like that. Or at least for now she loved him too much to castrate him.

*****

Cassie woke around midnight that night after she'd heard people talking outside. She laid in her bed a little while longer, trying to keep sleep from taking her again.

When she got out of bed Cassie slid into her slippers and then approached the window from which she'd heard the voices coming from. Her window was above the front porch, and when she opened it and looked down she saw Brent sitting in one of the rocking chairs her parents had loved to sit in.

Cassie shivered when she was hit with a gust of cool air from outside. Montana nights were always cold.

She looked back down at Brent. Brent only sat in those chairs when he needed to think about things. Cassie couldn't help but wonder what was on his mind.

Brent had ceased to realize that someone was watching or the fact that he hadn't heard her open up her window.

"Brent what are you doing sitting outside this late at night?" she asked not hiding the curiosity from her voice.

The sound of Cassie's voice startled Brent and he jumped in his chair, and then he began to search for the source of the voice he'd heard. Then he spotted Cassie's head sticking out of her window.

Brent got out of his chair and stood to look at Cassie. "Nothing. What are you doing up. I thought you were in bed asleep."

Cassie yawned as she spoke, "I was but I heard people talking outside of my window." She held her hand over her mouth to suppress yet another yawn. "Who were you talking to Brent?"

"One of the hands, he wanted to talk to me about something." Brent said trying hard not to reveal any information from his conversation with Clint.

Something was up with Brent. Normally he was upfront and honest about everything, but right now she felt like he was hiding something from her. Brent never hid things from her, but she didn't feel like trying to get the truth out of him at the moment.

"Okay, just don't stay up too late. Tomorrow's going to be a busy day around here." She said as she started to turn away from her window.

"Yes, mother." Brent said jokingly to Cassie, but she just ignored him and shut her window.

*****

Cassie hadn't been joking when she'd said that it was going to be a busy day around the ranch. Anna had been helping groom the horses all morning and it was tiring work. It was now around lunch time and Anna was famished. Hard work did that to a person.

Something had been off with Brent all morning. He'd been distant with everyone, and there also seemed to be some tension between the hands as well. And then there was Clint, he wouldn't keep I contact with anyone, and according to Cassie and he hadn't spent any time working with her. Anna was curious to find what was going on with all the males on the ranch.

Anna had always thought that females were supposed to be the moody ones, but according to the men on the ranch that thought wasn't true at all.

She stopped brushing one of the geldings and put the brush back into its container. Quickly she gave the horse an apple and gave him a little rub before exiting the stall to put the grooming supplies back up in the tack room.

As she walked out of the barn her stomach grumbled very unladylike. It was most definitely time for lunch.

The house was a bit little chilly thanks to it being autumn when she walked inside, so she quickly made a b-line for the thermostat to turn it up a couple of degrees.

Walking into the kitchen Anna thought about what to make for lunch. She didn't really want make sandwiches since it was cold and they'd be cold. After rummaging through the cabinets and the fridge she found the ingredients for grilled cheese and tomato soup. Both would be warm, perfect for a cold day lunch.

Just as she'd finished plating lunch, Cassie and Brent strolled into kitchen. Cassie took her plate to go, and if Anna was a betting woman, she'd bet that Cassie was going to go and have lunch with Clint, which meant that Anna would be stuck with enduring an awkward silence while eating her lunch with Brent.

They both sat down at the table to enjoy their meal. Brent sat across from her and just stared at her until his gaze dropped down to the bowl of soup sitting in front of him.

Anna couldn't handle the silence anymore. "What's going on around here?" she asked him and he just looked at her like he didn't understand a word she'd said. "You know with you and the ranch hands. You guys seem a little tense and moody."

He just stared at her with a blank expression on his face still. "I don't know what you're talking about."

Anna just sighed and ate another spoonful of her soup. "Sure you don't cowboy."

They sat in silence eating for a few more minutes.

Brent didn't mean to be so dense but if told her what was going on with the ranch hands then he'd be telling her something he'd told Clint he wouldn't tell anyone about. Plus, as he sat there and looked at her it became harder for him to figure out how to ask her out on the date he'd planned for the next night. He didn't know if he should straight up ask her to go on a date with him or to embellish it with pretty words that females seemed to love. Maybe he should just go with the first, and straight up ask her out. Didn't she say in her letter that she didn't like it when people beat around the bush?

Brent coughed to clear his throat. "Hey...Anna," she stopped eating her soup and looked up at him. "Well you know how tomorrow is Saturday?"

She nodded her head suspiciously. "Yeah."

Would you like to go dancing with me to the Broken String Tavern tomorrow night...you know like a date?" He blurted out and then immediately regretted it when he saw the look of surprise on her face.

Anna was stunned there was no other way to describe how she was currently feeling. The prospect of a date with Brent thrilled her, she still wanted to get to know him better, and this date was the perfect opportunity for her to do that.

"I'd love to."

*****

So I'm sorry for the wait on this chapter. I have been so busy lately and I just haven't had the time to right. My updates for the next couple of months will not be frequent, just bear with me. I'll get updates up just not as soon as you like.

Anyways, who feels bad for Cassie? I know, so do I, but if you want her to have her own story this has to happen. Things should be starting to heat up with Anna and Brent now/soon.

Thanks for reading! Enjoy! Please comment and vote!!!

Chapter 11

Chapter 11

The Broken String Tavern was a mass of people, everyone looking for a good time, a break from their day to day lives. It was the place where women gossiped about the available males, and men hung out with their buddies while drinking a couple beers, and getting a little rowdy.

They were lucky and managed to find a table without a problem. "Do you want a beer, or to dance first?" Brent asked while Anna sat down.

She'd warn the dress she'd gotten in town with a pair of brown leggings, and her boots. The perfect outfit if she did say so herself. Her hair was braided into a waterfall braid and the hair that wasn't part of the braid was curled loosely. Brent wore a nice pair of wranglers, and a cream colored shirt, which he'd, obviously had Cassie's help to pick it out because it matched her dress. He'd shinned his boots especially for their date, which Anna couldn't help but feel humbled by.

She smiled up at him. "You pick, both are fine with me."

Brent nodded his head and strolled over to the bar to get their beers. "Two Bud Lights, please," he called to the bartender.

Before he knew it he had the beers and was headed back to their table. He caught sight of Anna from a few feet away, and he lost his breath. She was stunning sitting there in her dress, her foot tapping in beat with the music.

Something about Anna had Brent wanting to take down all the walls he'd built up and show her his soft side, something he hadn't done since Leslie had shattered his heart.

He walked back to the table and tried to calm his raging heart.

*****

When Anna had looked up from tapping her foot along to the beat of the music she'd found Brent looking at her with a look of appreciation and want. She couldn't understand why he'd look at her in such a way. She was just plain Anna with the same features every other female had.

He came and sat the beers down and then he sat himself next to her.

Anna took a sip of the beer he'd gotten for her and tried to get the way he'd been looking at her out of her head. Could she hope that he was beginning to feel more than usual friendship for her? Because God knows that she felt more than friendship for him, way more.

The song changed and everyone began to dance a slow song. Anna gazed at the dance floor with longing. How she longed to have a man to hold her close while they danced to a romantic song, and know that he loved her and only her.

Brent must have noticed the look on her face because the next thing she knew she was, dancing with him on the floor, wrapped up in his embrace, praying that he would never let her go. They fit so perfectly together, it was like they had been made for one another.

Anna sighed her contempt, as she wound her arms around his neck and gently laid her head on his shoulder enjoying the moment. Brent began to twirl her around and Anna got lost in one of her little girl fantasies. Her prince was here and he was holding her and dancing with her, like she'd always dreamed.

One look up into his eyes and she was a goner. Brent was looking down on her with a look of wonder and adoring.

Call the press, Anna was losing her heart to this man.

With one precise movement Anna had moved her lips up to Brent's for a short kiss. Brent was momentarily shocked, but then he kissed her back as well. Everything that supposed to happen when you kiss the right person happened. The world faded away, and it was just the two of them with fireworks going off in the background.

Reluctantly they both pulled away, ending the kiss. Their eyes were glazed over with passion and desire from the kiss. Brent rested his forehead against hers and whispered down onto her face. "That was amazing."

A sigh escaped Anna's mouth while she tried to look up at him. "It was. Oh, Brent I don't want to be just friends with you anymore. I keep thinking about that kiss-"

He removed his forehead from hers. "You think about it too?" He asked, interrupting Anna.

"All night, and every time I look at you." He continued to shuffle them across the dance floor.

"Where do we go from here?" he asked while he gazed into her eyes.

"I don't know, but I do know that I'd like to start dating you seriously and see where all this goes."

"I'd like that too, but you should know I don't have the best past with relationships." He told her.

"I know you sister told me everything when we went into town, and none of it bothers me."

How did Brent get so lucky? This woman in his arms didn't care about his past; she just wanted to be part of his present, and future.

They became engrossed in each other while they danced to the music, and stared into each other's eyes, pondering what a future together could be like.

*****

After Clint learned about Brent's date with Anna, he figured that while they were in town would be the perfect time for him to tell Cassie that he was leaving. He was dreading the conversation more and more as the time approached.

He'd decorated their tree with fairy lights, and set up a picnic. Clint wanted his last night with Cassie to be memorable, he wanted to remember this night when he would get lonely and miss her, after he'd left.

Cassie was given specific instructions, to come to their tree at eight. Not a minute early, or late.

Just as Cassie was instructed she showed up on time. She was dressed in a beautiful denim button-up, but the back was made of a see through material, making it easy for him to see every part of her back that wasn't covered by her bra. The top of the back of the shirt was lace and the color of it matched the see through fabric. She wore a pair of skinny jeans that molded to her every curve with her brown equestrian riding boots on the outside. She was so stunning that Clint swallowed his tongue, and had a hell of a time getting his mouth to close.

Cassie quickly dismounted her horse, Murphy, and then tied his reins to one of the other trees nearby. Clint's gaze as Cassie walked over to him was filled with love and sadness. Cassie couldn't understand why he looked sad. If she was being perfectly honest, she suspected that he was going to propose.

"Hey, handsome," she smiled as she walked over to him. And look handsome he did, in his warn blue jeans, and flannel western shirt. His hair was slightly untamed from his Stetson. Cassie swore she'd never loved him more than in that moment.

He gave her a once over and then looked back into her eyes. "You look beautiful, Cassie."

She looked down at her feet to keep him from seeing her blush. "Clint you are so sweet sometimes." Slowly she looked up and then around at the picnic area he'd made for them. "What is all of this?" she questioned him while she motion to the picnic.

"I wanted to make tonight special." That comment alone had Cassie's heart beating a little faster.

The soft sound of Amazed by Lonestar played from a stereo Clint had set up. "Can I have this dance, Cassie?" He held out his hand to her.

She took it "Of course you can." He grabbed her and held her close. "I love you, Clint." Cassie whispered into his chest as they danced under the night sky.

Clint's heart broke just a little. She loved him yet he was leaving her.

No, he couldn't think about that. He had to just push that thought out of his head.

They danced, and danced. Their arms were around each other's waists as they shuffled their feet to the music.

Cassie felt contempt being held by the man she loved. She prayed that he'd propose to her because she wanted to be held in his arms like this every day for the rest of her life. This was home, the place she was always welcome and was always waiting for her. The place where no matter what happened she could count on and knew she was loved unconditionally.

A little while later the music faded away, and they separated, but Clint kept an arm around her waist as he led her to the blanket he'd set up for them. He sat down and she sat between his legs and leaned her head back on his chest. They gazed at the stars for a moment just enjoying being in each other's arms.

She tilted her face up and back so she could look at him. "Thank you for doing this Clint," Cassie said. "I'll never forget this night. You've made it so special."

He wrapped his arms around her waist, and then he pressed his chin to her shoulder while he said, "I'd do everything and anything for you. You're my whole world."

A smile crept across Cassie's face. "How can I not love you when you say such sweet things to me?"

"I don't know, but I do know that I love you, too." He kissed her lips gently. He was going to miss doing that. She tasted so sweet and feminine.

"Clint are we ever going to get married?" She paused collecting her thoughts, trying to figure out what she wanted to say to him. "I want to have your babies and go to sleep with you every night, and then wake up with you every morning. I want to make an honest living with you." She smiled sweetly up at Clint.

Panic shot through him. He couldn't do that for her, at least not yet. He shot up, leaving her flustered and sitting on the cold hard ground.

Something was wrong with him. "Clint are you okay? Clint you're worrying me, please talk to me." Now it was Cassie's turn to feel panicked.

He ran his hand across his face, trying to clear his thoughts so he could think clearly. "Cassie I can't. I can't not right now."

With that statement Cassie was up like a bolt, and she was madder than hell. "What do you mean you can't?" Her voice was rising to near hysteria. "You say you love me. Then why don't you marry me and we can have babies together, and just be happy for the rest of our lives?"

This was going to be harder than he thought. Maybe she would castrate him after all, she sure looked pissed enough to do so. "It's not that simple Cassie."

"What do you mean it's not that simple? Of course it's that simple, you love me, and I love you." Her voice went from near hysteria to a whisper.

"Cassie I can't give you what you need. You'd never be happy."

She looked up at him and her eyes were glistening with unshed tears. "Of course you can. Your love is all I need. It's all I'll ever need, I love you, Clint." Her voice kept breaking as she spoke.

"I love you, too, Cassie, but you'll need more than my love, and I can't give you that more." He paused getting his courage up so that he could tell her about his leaving. "That's why I need to leave-"

"What do you mean leave?" She interrupted him. Her arms were wound around her waist and she looked like a lost child. "I don't want you to leave."

He moved to hug her but she backed away from him. "Don't you dare hug me. I don't think I could handle that right now." Her heart was breaking at the moment, and him hugging her would just make it worse. Make the break her just that much more.

"I don't want to leave you baby-"

"Don't call me baby." She was crying now, sobs breaking loose. He just wanted to hug her and make her pain go away, but he couldn't, she wouldn't let him, and he felt defeated.

"Cassie you don't understand." That just made her mad. "I have to leave. I can't provide for you, I can't give you what you need, and God knows that I want to do that. That's why I have to leave."

None of this was making sense to her. That wasn't true, she understood that he was leaving her and just that thought blocked out everything else.

Oh God, he was leaving her.

How could he do this to her? How could he be so cruel?

"You want to leave me," she whispered as she stood there staring at him.

Oh, God he really was a monster, he was hurting her.

He stepped towards her. "Not for long, Cassie, just until I can make enough to provide for you."

"You don't need to provide for me. I can provide for myself just fine."

"I know you can, but I'm the man, Cassie. I need to able to do that for you." He was pacing, now. She wasn't listening to him or trying to understand what he was trying to say to her.

She was done. If he wanted to leave her, then fine she'd let him. She didn't need him anyways.

"Fine then leave me. God am I really that terrible, that you want to leave me?" She yelled at him.

"It's not that way Cassie." He was trying to reason with her.

"Oh, I think it is." She pointed at herself. "I don't need you. Just leave. Let me be real clear." She enunciated her words. "I never want to see you again, and if I do, I will not be reliable for my actions. If you ever come back I will never forgive you, and don't think that with a few pretty words I will fall at your feet. I am through with you. Good riddance."

With that she strode away from him, and she did not look back. Looking back would just bring her pain. She went and untied Murphy's reins, and then she mounted his back.

The tears finally began to fall once she was out of sight of Clint.

Damn that man!

How dare he leave her. Well she wasn't going to waste another moment of her life on him. She wiped the tears off her cheeks. From now on she'd never let another man get as close to her as she let Clint, ever again.

*****

That certainly hadn't gone the way Clint had planned. She wouldn't even listen to him. He could try and go after her, the only problem was that she wouldn't listen to him, and he'd probably end up losing an important part of his anatomy.

What he really needed to do was pack all this stuff back up, head back to the ranch, hook up his horse trailer to his truck. Then he would load his horse up, and grab all his belongings from the house he'd been living in, put it in the back of his tuck and leave.

He needed to start earning money so that he could get back here faster, and convince Cassie to marry him. He had the feeling the road ahead of him was going to be long and hard, maybe even a little bumpy too. But he'd survive it, and then Cassie would be his wife, the mother of his children.

Those would be the days. He would be able to look at her and know that she was his wife, and he would be able to see her hold his child. That was his dream, to see Cassie hold his baby in her arms and gaze at him and the child with so much love that she would burst with it.

It would happen someday. For now he needed to leave, to get out of this place as soon as possible.

*****

All the way back to the ranch Anna and Brent held hands. They both were happy with their new found relationship. Anna was sure that she had been glowing for the rest of their date. They'd danced the whole time, during the slow songs they were wrapped up in each other's arms, and during the fast ones she found that Brent had two left feet, but she didn't mind that at all, not one little bit. She actually found it quite endearing.

They happiness only broken when they got back to the ranch house, and found Cassie sitting on the front steps sobbing hysterically.

Anna immediately ran to her. Seeing Cassie in tears hurt Anna's heart, she was like a sister to Anna.

Anna grabbed Cassie's arm lightly to get her attention. "Oh, honey what happened?"

Cassie slightly looked up at her. "He...l-left...me-e." She said between the sobs that racked her body.

"Who left you, Cassie?" Anna had no clue what she was talking about.

"Cli-int, he sa-said that he-he couldn't s-stay here wi-with me."

Anna's heart broke for her a little. "Oh, Cassie I'm so sorry." She tried to help Cassie to her feet. "let's go inside and then you can tell me what happened."

Brent was behind them, as Anna led Cassie up the stairs to her room.

With one swift move Anna pulled back the covers, and then helped Cassie take off her boots.

Once she was in her bed Anna and Brent coerced the story of what had happened that night out of Cassie.

Brent had wanted to leave and find Clint, and smash his fist into Clint's face a time, or two or maybe until the fool was unconscious.

Luckily enough Anna and Cassie had convinced him that he didn't want his own fool neck to end up in jail for assault.

Brent left Cassie's room while Anna helped Cassie change for bed. He wasn't far away though; he waited in the hallway for Anna to emerge.

He felt so bad for his little sister; he never wanted to see Cassie cry over any man. He wanted to kill Clint for putting her through this pain. This was why he'd made that rule. None of the ranch hands were supposed to date his little sister for precisely this reason. He never wanted to see her hurt this much, and yet here he was outside of her room listening to Anna trying to calm her while sobs coursed through her body.

If he ever saw Clint again he would give him a piece of his mind. No one would hurt his baby sister ever again, at least not if he ever had anything to do about it.

A little while later after Cassie had cried herself to sleep, Anna emerged from the room. Brent was there waiting for her. He held out his arms for her, and she went to her and laid her head on his chest. He wrapped his arms around her waist and she did the same to him.

"Do you think she'll get better." He whispered into Anna's ear.

She sighed and shivered from the feel of his breath on her skin. "I don't know."

*****

So that was quite a shocker! Poor Cassie. Don't be too mad at Clint though, he's just trying to be what she needs, and leaving and making something out of himself is something that he has to do before he can marry her.

The good news is that Brent and Anna are finally together, and also that Cassie and Clint will now get their own story.

The song on the side is Amazed by Lonestar. It's the song that Clint and Cassie danced to. It's a beautiful song if you ask me. Sorry it took so long for me to get this chapter up, but it was a tough and long one to write. I hope you enjoy!!! Please vote and comment!!!

Chapter 12

Chapter 12

It'd been a little under a month since Clint had left Cassie. Every day her broken heart healed a little more. Cassie was still completely shattered on the inside.

Brent felt helpless as he watched his sister try to heal her broken heart. The first week they couldn't get her out of her room. You would have thought she was mourning Clint's death, and she might as well have been. Her love was gone and they had no clue when he would come back, or if he even would after the talking to Cassie had given him.

Everyday Cassie had trouble understanding why Clint had wanted to leave. Nothing made sense to her anymore. She walked around in a fog trying to fight her way through it, but she just kept getting pushed farther and farther back. The only thing that seemed to help her was when she would ride Murphy for hours on end. No one knew where she went and Cassie was okay with that, she wanted to spend as much time as she could at her and Clint's tree.

Anna had hope that in time Cassie's heart would completely heal. Although, she honestly didn't believe her heart would be fully healed until she had Clint back. Brent had tried to figure out where Clint had gone, but each time he'd find something it would lead him to a dead end. Every time he heard Cassie crying he looked like someone had physically punched him in the stomach.

While Cassie had been broken apart, Brent and Anna had been getting closer. Every free moment they'd had they spent together. Just the other night they'd been snuggled up on the couch watching a movie while they shared a bowl of popcorn. Brent at heart was a complete and utter teddy bear. He still had that this-is-my-woman-and-I-will-protect-her attitude, but when you really got to know him that was just one of the many things that made Brent, Brent.

Since it was a week before Thanksgiving Brent's parents would be arriving the next day to spend the holiday with them.

Anna was extremely nervous to meet his parents. They didn't exactly have a normal relationship, especially not if you think about how they met. From everything she'd heard from Cassie told her that they were amazing people. Anna just hoped that they liked her.

"What are you thinking about, Anna Banana." She loved it when Brent called her that.

She smiled over at him from the top of Cupid. "Nothing really, well, actually I'm a bit nervous about meeting your parents tomorrow."

"Don't worry about it they'll love you," Brent reached out to hold her hand in his.

"But how do you know they will, they've never met me before." Anna wasn't as convinced as Brent was at the situation.

"Anna there are something's I just know, okay?" He asked her while she stared off into the setting sun.

"Okay, I trust you."

That one statement meant the world to him. Brent knew about what her parents had done to her, and knowing that she could trust him after all she been through made him like her all the more.

"Thank you for trusting me," he squeezed her hand lightly with his. "Let's get back to the ranch. I don't want to leave Cassie there alone for too long."

Anna gripped Cupid's reigns a little tighter. "I'll race you," she said as she worked as she shot off on Cupid. Brent could hear her laughing as he realized she'd cheated. With a quick yank on his reigns he got Mav up to a gallop. Cupid was fast, but Mav was just a faster and it took him no time to catch up with Anna.

"Nice try Anna Banana," He smirked over at her while they galloped. "I'll see you back at the ranch." With that he made Maverick go a little faster, but he still kept Anna about five yards behind him the whole way back to the ranch.

*****

"I can't believe you beat me," Anna said as she dismounted Cupid in front of the barn.

"What else was I supposed to do, you cheated?"

With Cupid's reign in her had she playfully smacked him on the shoulder with her hand that was free. "Of course I had to cheat, or else I never would have gotten in front of you."

"Well, that is definitely true." Brent looked at her with a sly grin on his face.

"Ouch, that was mean," she elbowed him in the ribs and he broke into a fit of laughter coming from deep within his belly. She loved the way he laughed; it was quite sexy if you asked her.

"Okay let's get Cupid and Mav inside before I elbow you again for laughing at me." Anna grabbed Mav's reigns as well as she walked into the barn leaving Brent to control his laughter on his own.

Anna put Mav in his stall first, and then she took Cupid to his own. She didn't worry about rubbing Mav down because she knew Brent would do it once he was done laughing at her.

Cupid happily ate his apple after he'd been rubbed down. Anna was waiting at Mav's stall, finished with rubbing Cupid down when Brent came in to get Mav situated.

"Did you have a nice laugh?" She asked him.

"I'm not gonna lie, it was pretty nice. I haven't laughed like that in a long time."

"Well, I'm glad I could make your life a little better." Her arms were crossed over her chest as she smile at him.

"Oh, you've made it way better in the past month," he smiled at her and grabbed her by the waist.

Anna couldn't help the blush that spread over her cheeks from his words, and his touch. "I'm glad you think so." She smiled coyly up at him. "Now why don't you kiss me?"

"I thought you'd never ask."

With a smile on his lips Brent bent his head down to kiss Anna good and proper. Brent had never felt anything as right as kissing Anna. That though scared him just a little on the inside. He wasn't ready to commit, or settle down. He needed more time to wrap his head around everything.

When they broke apart their eyes were a little glazed over with the passion from the kiss they'd shared. Their lips were swollen from the kiss as well. Anna brought a hand to her lips and smiled shyly at Brent.

Brent cleared his throat. "I think that we should probably rub Mav down, he doesn't look like he's too happy with me right now."

"I think your right. I wouldn't want Mav to be angry." She looked over at Mav. "Huh, boy you don't want to be angry, you just want to be rubbed down after your long ride?"

With a lift of his head Mav nodded, yes at Anna. "I think we have our answer, Brent. Why don't you rub him down while I get all the horses each an apple?" Mav's ears perked up when he heard the word, apple. Anna couldn't help but giggle at him. Mav and Brent were the same, each tough on the outside, but big teddy bears on the inside.

"Sounds good." Mav neighed making Brent move his attention away from Anna. "Okay, don't be cranky; I'm coming to rub you down right now."

There was a small area in the barn where they kept the feed for the horses, and it included multiple deep sinks where they refilled the buckets for the horses water. There was even a small fridge where they kept carrots and apples for the horses.

Anna grabbed one of the bags of apples, and then shut the door to the fridge. She went down the rows patting each of the horses and giving them an apple. She spent a little more time with Cupid because he was her horse, and she wanted to give him a little extra love.

It took a little over fifteen minutes to get the horses their apples. She made it back over to Mav's stall with the last apple in her hand. She couldn't help but smile at the sight she found. Brent had his head bent towards Mav's as he whispered soothingly to the horse while he brushed him.

There was truly nothing like a man and his horse, Brent and Mav were the perfect example of that.

Mav noticed her first, and he raised his head to look at her. The apple in Anna's hand immediately gained his attention, and he started to move away from Brent and towards the apple. That was when Brent caught on, he looked up and when he saw her, he smiled.

"Look there," he said to Mav. "Someone's got a treat for you." Mav looked at Brent for his approval to go and get the apple. "Well go and get it," he told Mav.

Anna moved into the stall and held out her palm with the apple on it. Mav ate the apple greedily. You'd have thought he'd never had an apple before or a treat for that matter.

"Do you ever give this horse treats?" Anna asked as she gave Brent an accusing look.

"I do, but at the site of a treat he'll throw me under the bus any day." He shot Mav a glare and the horse glared back at him and went on chomping the last of his apple. "See I told you so. Did you see that glare?"

She couldn't help the laugh that came out. "I did. You two are so alike and you don't even realize it."

Brent looked at her funny. "Did you just call me a horse?"

"Nope. I just said that you two are very alike." Anna shot him a sheepish smile.

"Uh, huh." He grabbed her by the waist. "I don't believe you.

"Oh, you don't, do you?" She put her hands over his, which were situated on her waist. "Well what are you going to do about it?"

"I haven't decided yet. I'm going between tickling," he ran his fingertips lightly up her sides making her giggle slightly.

"No don't do that," Anna begged him. "I hate being tickled."

"That's good to know," he stated. "Or I could kiss you senseless here in the barn with all the horses watching us." He brought her face towards his.

"I think I like the second option better," she whispered over his lips.

"I think I do, too."

Very tentatively at first he ran his lips over hers, just tasting her slightly. Anna didn't want a slow and sweet kiss. She wanted a hot, fast and steamy one. She pressed her lips harder against his eliciting a moan from both of them. Brent was okay with the change in pace as long as it was what Anna wanted.

They stood their kissing each other for a while, until someone standing feet away from them cleared their throat.

Anna broke her lips away from Brent's and then she looked up. She found two people standing near them. The woman looked a lot like Cassie, and then it hit her.

Oh God! His parents had just found them sharing a very, and she meant very, passionate kiss.

Brent kept one arm protectively round Anna's waist. "Hi, mom and dad."

Now Anna wasn't one to faint, but she couldn't help it when everything went black and she slumped against Brent.

*****

So someone got to meet the parents... I'm not gonna lie if the first time I met the guy I was involved with's parents like that I probably would have fainted too. I think that the song on the side fits how Cassie is feeling right now perfectly. It's, Can't Shake You by Gloriana, please give it a listen, I hope you like it! I know that I love it!

Sorry it took so long for me to update. I'm still really busy right now so updates will still be irregular and stretched far apart. I'll try for at least one update a month, but that might not happen.

I hope you enjoyed this chapter!!!!! Please comment and vote!!!

Chapter 13

Chapter 13

Anna opened her eyes and looked around. Her vision was little blurry when she looked around, but she quickly came to realize that she was in her room. The only problem was that she had no clue what had happened. The last thing she remembered was being in the barn with Brent and Mav.

A face came into Anna's view, and she recognized it immediately, it was Brent's mothers. Anna let out a groan. That's when it all came flooding back to her. The kiss. How she'd fainted after seeing his parents for the first time. God, she felt like a fool.

"It's good to see those eyes of yours open, dear." His mother said. "You had us all worried when you fainted on my son. I think Brent was worried the most," she smiled to herself. "I think Brent was worried the most, he started barking orders at everyone immediately. He carried you to the house and put you in your bed..." She paused. 'I'll bet you that he's standing out in the hall pacing right this minute, worried about you."

Anna put her palm on her forehead and began to sit up, and as she did so she let out another groan. "I'm so embarrassed," she shook her head. "I can't believe I fainted."

"Now don't you be embarrassed, we were just worried about you, that's all."

"But you saw me kissing," Anna blushed a crimson red color, "your son, and then I fainted. How can that not be embarrassing?"

Brent's mother laughed a little. "There are things that are far more embarrassing, than meeting a man's mother after a...kiss, and then promptly fainting. After all when I met Brent's grandparents I tripped face first into a mud puddle," she sighed. "I was so mortified. I quickly stood up and wiped the mud off my hands, and then I shook his grandpa's hand and then I gave his grandma a hug." She let out a sigh and then a giggle. "I covered her in mud!"

They both laughed a little at the story his mother had just told.

"Thank you for making me feel a little better." Anna smiled a thank you smile at her. "If you don't mind me asking, what's your name or what should I call you? I mean Brent's mentioned you guys, but always as his parents, or mom and dad."

She patted Anna's leg. "Well, I'm Denise, and their father's name is William, but everyone calls him Bill. You can call me Denise, and him Bill, for now at least." Denise looked at Anna with a knowing look.

The blush that Anna had been sporting just a minute before came back, but now not only was it on her face but it spread to her ears and neck. She couldn't believe that Denise had just been so open about that.

"Oh, don't get embarrassed, dear. My son loves you; I just don't think he knows it yet." Denise gave her an appreciative look, "and if that blush is any indication you're starting to feel the same way, too."

Anna began to shift uncomfortably on the bed, becoming extremely more uncomfortable as the time passed. She wasn't quite sure she liked talking with Brent's mother about their romantic relationship. Though, they hadn't gone farther than a few heated kisses, it just didn't feel or seem right.

"I should probably stop before I get even more ahead of myself, shouldn't I?"

"I think that would be good." Anna got up off the bed. "We should probably go downstairs now. I think they're probably a little anxious waiting to see if I'm okay, and I just want to assure them that I'm fine." Denise rose after Anna and then they left for the living room together.

Everyone was in the living room when they got downstairs. Brent was sitting on the loveseat waiting for her to join him as he'd done countless nights before. Cassie was in the recliner all curled up, and Bill-much like Brent had done with Anna-was waiting for Denise to join him.

Before Anna had a chance to sit down Bill rose and shook her hand. "It's nice to meet you."

Anna touched a piece of hair behind her ear and replied as she sat down next to Brent. "Thank you. It's great to finally meet Brent's parents." She looked over at Brent and he smiled at her.

When Cassie saw Brent smile at Anna adoringly she crawled up into an even smaller ball. It looked like she was about to cry. Denise looked over at her youngest child and was immediately worried no one had said anything about Cassie not being her usual self. But that look made Denise want to go and hold her baby while she whispered soothing words to her, and so that's what she did.

"Oh, baby girl, what's wrong," Denise cooed as she walked over to her daughter. By then everyone had noticed that Anna was close to tears. Both Brent and his father looked like they wanted to be sick, and Anna wanted to help comfort her, but she knew that Denise would do a far better job than she could.

One silent tear rolled down Cassie's face as her mother sat down next her. The comfort of being held by her mother broke the last of her resolve, the tears just flowed, unable to be stopped by anything or anyone.

"Shhh...it's okay. Momma's here. Don't worry, whatever it is it will be okay." Cassie was crying silent tears into her mother's chest. When she heard that it would be okay she broke into sobs. "Oh, Cassie I really wish you would tell me what's wrong."

Cassie laid there for several more minutes while Denise continued to coo to her before she spoke. "It...it won't be...be oh...okay. He le...left me... I love...him...and he left...me."

One look at Bill's face told everyone that he wanted to kill whoever had hurt his little girl.

"Who left you, baby?" Denise asked while she rubbed Cassie's back soothingly.

"Cli...Clint." Bill and Denise both looked over at Brent and Anna obviously wanting answers to whom this Clint character was, and why he'd left their daughter in pieces.

Brent just shrugged his shoulders. "I didn't even know that she was dating someone until we got back from our date and found her crying, saying that he'd left her." Brent sighed and Anna held onto his arm. "He used to work here, he was a great guy-"

"A great guy?!" Bill boomed, clearly not happy with Brent's choice of words. "How could he be a great guy when he did this to your sister?"

Brent tried to speech, but Cassie wiped her eyes and looked up at her father. "Daddy he was a great guy. He told me that he had to leave, and make something out of himself. He thought that he could never be good enough for me if he was just a ranch hand."

"Well, that's just stupid," Bill told Cassie. "Your grandpa wasn't much more than a ranch hand when he met you grandmamma, and he built this ranch up to what it is today with the help of her."

"I know that," Cassie's head was still resting on her mother. "But Clint doesn't understand that we could do that together."

"I'd like to teach this young man a lesson, but I can tell none of you know where he is, or else he'd be in a hospital because of what Brent would have done to him.

"I really don't want to talk about him anymore." Everyone nodded in agreement. "That part of my life is over, and I want it to stay that way."

*****

It seemed like after Cassie admitted that she was done with Clint, she started to make even more progress on healing her broken heart every day. No one heard her crying at night, there would just be a few sniffles every now and again when she'd think of something that was related to Clint. Brent now longer wanted Clint's blood just maybe one or two decent blows to his stomach.

Cassie's father however, seemed like he would never be able to forget Clint hurting his daughter. Anna believed that if Clint ever came back he would have the hardest time winning Bill over and not Cassie.

A week had passed and the more Anna had gotten to know Brent's parents, the more she began to love them. Denise told her countless times that she would make Brent a wonderful wife...someday at least. Neither of them were anywhere near that point in their relationship.

Although, Anna couldn't deny that every day she got closer to falling for Brent, not mention wanting kids, a home... really she wanted the whole nine yards.

One day out riding, Anna had confessed to Denise how much she loved to write, and she'd even let her read the book she'd written in college. Never before had she let anyone read it, but Denise felt like a mother to her and so she'd wanted to share it with her. Denise had showered her with her appraisal of how much she loved the book, and even encouraged Anna to get it published, saying that she thought it could be one of the great American novels. Anna didn't think that would ever happen, but she was happy to have her support. Anna had promised Denise that she would tell Brent about her love for writing and let him read her work but just not...now. Maybe in a month or two when she felt their relationship was a little more developed and secure.

Thanksgiving was tomorrow and Anna felt so honored that she was going to be able to partake in their family traditions. As it was, they'd already baked a few pies and an assortment of other things today. Cassie had a knack for baking which Anna was quite happy to learn because if she was telling the truth, she too loved to bake.

"What are you thinking about?" Brent asked Anna as they they'd on the couch after everyone else had gone to bed.

Anna had gotten so wrapped up in her thoughts that she'd forgotten about how Brent was snuggling her in his arms. "Nothing really... Just about the future, and everything else, I guess."

"Am I in those plans for the future?"

Anna looked up into Brent's eyes and she could tell that he truly wanted to know the answer. "Of course, but only if you want to be." She said shyly to him.

"I do. I hope to be there for a lot of it."

She couldn't help the smile that spread across her face. How could she have gotten so lucky? And it was all because she answered an ad. Falling in love with this man was possibly the easiest task Anna had ever had in her life.

"I'm glad you said that. I don't think I can ever imagine my life without you, Cassie, or your parents ever again."

"Why don't you ever talk about your family?" Brent asked out of the blue.

Brent immediately felt Anna stiffen in his arms, she hadn't been expecting that. "You know why I don't."

"Yeah, but you've only told me part of it, not the whole story."

"It's hard to talk about it," she sighed out in frustration.

"I know it is, but I want you to be able to tell me everything. And if that means I have to break down the walls where your family is concerned then I'll do it." He kissed Anna's temple, and she sighed in contemp. "I just want you to know that you can trust me with anything. I've never had a ton of trust in my prior relationships, but I want to have that trust with you. No one but you."

Anna wanted that too, but she didn't know how to tell Brent that. So she'd just have to show him. "Well, growing up I had the perfect family life that was until I decided that I wanted to pursue a writing career in the city." She paused finding it hard trying to think of the right thing to say. "I realize now that the city was never right for me, and that I could have my career living anywhere I wanted to. Well, my father got angry because he hates how corrupt the city is, so he convinced my mother that as long as I wanted to live somewhere with mostly no values or broken ones then I could be a part of their family."

Anna's throught was getting clogged with emotion as she began to speak again. "I didn't want to have to settle for else, when I knew I could be more, so I left and went to college which I somehow managed to pay for. I realized that they were right about the city, but not me. I wasn't going to go back home because then, well then they would tell me I was wrong, which I wasn't. I had to learn the lesson on my own, but I won't... and I mean I won't regret it because it led me to who I'm today and helped me to realize how much I really love to write, and all I can do is be happy for that."

Anna realized that she'd been rambling, but she didn't care. It had felt so good to get all of that off of her mind. She felt like a new woman.

It felt like there was a brick sitting in the bottom of his stomach. He'd never thought that her parents had made her fell like a failure; he'd believed that they'd just disowned her and nothing else. He was angry at her parents. Angry at them for not believing in her. Angry at them for making her fell like a failure. Angry at them for every time they'd made her cry-just like she was doing now.

Brent let out a defeated sigh; he was not good at consoling woman. "I'm so sorry that they made you feel like a failure." He kissed her on the forehead and then lightly on the tip of her nose, trying to help comfort her. "The only problem is that I can't be too angry at them because if they'd never have done all the stuff that they did, I'd never of gotten to have you."

*****

Sorry about the lack of an update for about a month and a half now. Life's just gotten away from me, and I've had a lot of issues and drama with my family. Anyways, I just wanted to say that I'm back and to expect another update in probably another week or so.

The song on the side is amazing and I think that it relates to this chapter. Give it a listen. I promise that you won't be disappointed! Jo Dee Messina is some of country music at its finest! I considered using Celine Dion's version, but I like this one better, and no hate for that!

Have a great rest of the night, or morning wherever you're at. I hope you enjoy!!! If you do please vote and leave a comment! You guys are the people that keep me going when I loose my confidence in my writing!!! Reading your comments and seeing you guys vote, always helps to bring me back to my writing!!!

Chapter 14

Chapter 14

"I wish you guys could stay longer. I've really enjoyed getting to know you both." Anna smiled at Brent's parents as they got ready to leave for Wyoming.

Denise smiled at Anna and gave her a hug. "We'll miss you, too, but we'll be back in a month for Christmas. At least that is if my son hasn't run you off yet."

Brent let out a groan and started after his mother. "Really mom, really."

Bill decided to break in now. "Denise was that really necessary? Couldn't you just leave the poor boy alone?"

Cassie and Anna were huddled together to the side giggling to themselves.

Denise playfully smacked Bill's arm. "Of course not. What kind of mother would I be if I didn't embarrass my kids?"

A goofy grin appeared on Brent's face. "The good kind."

"Oh, you hush up." She lightly smacked him on the arm. "Now why don't you give your mother a hug?"

Brent reluctantly moved into her arms and then he gave Denise a bone crushing hug. "I love you ma'."

"Oh, I love you, too son. No give you father a hug, or whatever you men do."

As Brent moved to give his father a manly hug, Denise moved toward Cassie and Anna.

First Denise approached Cassie and gave her a hug. As they were holding each other Denise spoke, "I love you so much Cass. Don't let anyone get you down. I know you loved that boy, but he's not worth it if all he's doing is hurting you and bringing you down."

Cassie nodded her headed slowly at her mother while her eyes were glazed over with fresh tears ready to spill at a moment's notice. Denise kissed her on the cheek and then she walked over to Anna.

"I know my son is going to love you, just give him a little time." Denise whispered in her ear so that no one else could hear her. "I know you're halfway in love with him, too."

There was a look of shock on Anna's face after Denise finished whispering in her ear. "How did you know? Did I show any signs? Oh, goodness don't tell Brent, I don't want him to freak out. We haven't known each other that long." By the end she was rambling and Denise was having a hard time keeping up with her.

"Don't worry I won't tell him. Be good you're already like a daughter to me." Denise paused unsure if she should continue. "He's more stubborn than anyone I know. He's going to think that he's not deserving of your love, but just give him time. He'll believe you someday, okay?"

Anna nodded taking in all of the information that she was told. "Thank you for being a mom to me."

"No problem, just remember everything I told you." Denise hugged her one last time and then she headed over to her husband and her son.

"What was that all about?" Brent asked, he and his father both had curious looks on their faces.

"Nothing for you to worry about." Denise turned towards her husband. "Let's get going, we need to get back to Wyoming. As they head to their car they waved at all of the kids. Because that's what they all were they were their kids. No matter if they shared the same blood or bound by blood, both of those things would come soon enough. Or that's at least what Denise thought.

*****

Anna walked into the house after they could no longer see Brent's parents. She was surprised that Denise had figured out everything in the short time she'd known Anna. It was probably mother's intuition like everyone talks about.

It was one hundred percent true, too. Anna Douglas was half way in love with Brent and moving farther towards being in love with him every day.

Brent walked up behind her. "So... What'd my mother say to you?"

Anna turned around to face him. "Some things are meant to stay between women, and for men to never find out."

As Brent was talking he groaned. "Come on, I'm curious. I'm a guy."

"I know you are, but that still doesn't change the fact that I'm not going to tell you anything."

"Please." He said extending the 'e'.

"Nope, it's not going too happened." Anna giggled when Brent put his hands on the ticklish spot on her side.

"What if I tickle you?" He rubbed his hands over her side, but she still nodded her head no. "No. Okay, then what if I kiss you senseless?" Anna shook her head no again, but Brent wasn't listening. He pulled her in close and began to kiss her hungrily. Not listening to her protests, just kissing her until she ached with a need for him that she'd never felt for anyone before, but she couldn't let it go that far. Neither one of them was ready for anything like that.

Anna pulled her mouth away from Brent's. "No, Brent we can't do this. Neither of us is ready for this." She rested her head against his chest.

Brent sighed and kissed her forehead tenderly. "I'm sorry I kind of lost control there."

"It's okay, it was nice, just a little too fast."

Brent ran a hand over his face and then he looked down at his boots. "Uh... I think I'll just go outside and check on everything."

Anna smiled, he was so cute when he was embarrassed. "Okay, lunch will be around twelve thirty. I'll be waiting for you."

*****

The cool air hit Cassie as she sat atop Murphy with a hand held to her stomach. Cassie now knew that she would be okay. After her parents had left she'd gone into the bathroom and threw up her breakfast, which had been happening for the past week.

Cassie had missed her period the prior month, and she'd began to wonder if she was indeed carrying Clint's baby in her tummy. Throwing up for a week and the fact that she was nauseous half of the time made her sure that she was pregnant.

Maybe it was selfish of Cassie, but she hoped her baby was a boy. She wanted a man in her life without all of the work of having a husband.

This baby was just the thing to bring her out of the deep depression that had been lurking over her since Clint had left her.

Cassie was going to try once more to look for Clint, but she didn't think she'd find him. Last time she'd tried she'd come up with nothing, but she had to at least try and find him. Try and tell him that they were having a son. Try and tell him that she didn't care if he didn't have a penny to his name. Cassie just wanted him for the sake of him being himself.

She just had to find a way to tell him. She didn't want to be like those women that used their children as pawns with the fathers'. Using them to get what they wanted. There was no way in hell that she would ever do that.

There was no way that she was going to hide this baby from his father. The only problem was that she didn't know if she could help it. She didn't know if she'd be able find him. Her chances of being able to find him and tell him about their son were slim to null.

The other bridge that she had to cross was telling her family about the little one that was currently growing in her tummy, waiting for the day he would show his face to the world.

*****

Anna stood by the window in the kitchen while she looked out onto the vast Donovan spread. She'd seen the bulge in Brent's pants, and she couldn't deny the satisfaction she'd felt. Now she wasn't a tease nor had she ever been, but she'd enjoyed knowing Brent wanted her because she'd never wanted anyone or anything more in her life.

Although Anna wanted all of that with Brent, she knew that they couldn't it was too soon, and there was the fact that neither of them were ready for that. Oh, but she wanted him alright. Maybe in a few weeks when their relationship was stronger, more matured. Not to mention the fact that she wanted their first time to be when she knew she was one-hundred percent irreversibly in love in love with him.

Call her old fashioned, but she believed in true love, and even though she hadn't waited for the one. She wanted things to be right with Brent, even if they weren't exactly conventional. She never all about the bad love making, and she wanted it to be good-right with Brent.

It was only going to take Anna a couple of minutes to fix everyone's lunch so she went took her laptop onto the porch and sat in the cool autumn air.

She'd been sitting there so long writing and editing something that she'd been on, that she didn't notice when Cassie walked onto the porch with a hand on her tummy and a goofy grin plastered to her face.

"Hey, Anna." Cassie's smile as bright and radiant as Anna had ever seen it.

Anna looked up at Cassie. "Hi, what's got you so happy?"

Cassie kept her hand rested on her stomach. "Guess..."

"What! No, I'm terrible at guessing and you know that." Anna had a goofy grin plastered to her face, too. "Now tell me!"

"I don't know, I'm kind of enjoying making you squirm."

"Stop...! Tell me...!" Anna squealed.

"Fine... Alright, alright! I'll tell you!" The she hesitated for a second.

"Stop stalling."

Cassie looked at her hand and then spoke. "I'm-"

That's when it hit Anna. "Oh my God you're pregnant!" Anna once again squealed.

Cassie kept smiling at Anna and didn't say a word.

"You really are aren't you?"

Cassie smiled and giddily nodded her head yes.

Anna set her laptop down and stood up and started to jump around excitedly. It was a couple of minutes until she could calm herself down enough to stop jumping around.

"Anna, I'm so happy. When Clint left I never thought that I'd ever feel happiness again, but I've never been so happy. I have his baby growing in me."

Anna now looked at Cassie with a skeptical look on her face. "Are you one-hundred percent sure you're pregnant? Have you taken a pregnancy test, yet?"

The smile left Cassie's face. "Well, no, but I feel it. I don't know how I do, but I just know that I'm pregnant with Clint's baby." Another dreamy look made its way onto Cassie's face. "I'm going to look for him again, Anna. I want him to know about are son-"

"What!" Anna interrupted her. "How do you know you're having a boy?!"

"Well I don't." She looked at Anna sheepishly. "I just feel like I am. Anyw ays... Maybe if he knows about the baby he'll come home and be with me."

"How about this," Anna suggested. "How about we go into town buy a couple pregnancy tests, and if they come up positive then we'll go to your doctor and you can take one of their tests, and we can get you some prenatal care."

"Anna..." Cassie groaned. "I don't need to take tests, I already know."

"Fine, but humor me." Anna held her hand up to Cassie to stop her from interrupting. "And then we can go on from there. Why take the chance of getting your heart broken again if there really is no child?"

"Okay fine... We'll do it your way, but just so you know, there is a child growing in me." Cassie looked at Anna stubbornly.

"Fine, but were still doing it my way," Anna said triumphantly. "We better make Brent some lunch, and leave him a note saying where we are before we leave."

"Yes, mother hen." Cassie said with a grin plastered to her face.

"Oh you hush up," Anna huffed. "I am so not a mother hen and you know it."

*****

So... I've been gone for two weeks... I'm sorry, I know that I said this would be up a week earlier, but I got so busy, and yeah. So here it is, better late than never. Right? More drama is going to becoming in the next few chapters...

I also have the title of Cassie's story to share with you. Dun.. Dun... Duhhh... It's Runaway Bride! Ah, I'm so excited

Anyways, well, now you guys have a hint as to what a bit of the drama in Cassie's story is going to be about. I think the song on the side is great for Cassie at this moment. She's out of her mild depression and back into the world of the living. Personally I love Tim McGraw and Let it Go is a song of his that I really like.

If you like it please vote and comment!!! Thank you for taking the time to read this!!!

Chapter 15

Chapter 15

Anna and Cassie made sure to leave a note and tell the hands where they were going since Brent was nowhere to be found.

It took a little while to get into town, but since it had been barely noon when they left they managed to get into town a little after one. The first place they went was the pharmacy. They had to get the pregnancy tests and then they were going to find a bathroom so that Cassie could use them.

They managed to find the tests without a problem, but when you live near a small town, everyone knows you, and when you do something as scandalous as buy a pregnancy tests, they have questions... All the woman would wonder who it was that had got themselves knocked up, and the all the guys would wonder who got lucky.

"Let's find a bathroom where we can go and have you use the tests." Anna spoke up.

Cassie looked nervously at Anna. "I don't want to do this in public. It's already nerve racking enough knowing that there is about a ninety-nine percent chance that I'm pregnant."

"Okay, then where do you suggest we go?"

"I don't know maybe somewhere private."

Anna sighed and looked sternly at Cassie. "You see Cassie I don't exactly know anywhere private we can go in town. If you've forgotten, I'm kind of new here. So you wanna help me out?"

Well, I have a friend who owns a store here in town and the bathroom in her store is in the backroom of her store. So it's pretty private."

Anna looked relieved. "Okay, where's her store? Can I get a name for her and the store?"

"The store's a couple blocks down Main Street. It's called Jess's Old Time Boutique, and I'm guessing you know what her name is, just from that."

"Yup." Anna grabbed Cassie's hand and pulled her out of the town pharmacy and out into the parking lot.

"Seriously did you have to pull me out of there like I was a two year old or something." Cassie asked Anna incredulously.

"No, but you'll probably have one in a couple of years."

"Hey, hey. No reason to get all personal here." Cassie sighed with a look of shock on her face. "I thought we were friends," she pouted.

Anna couldn't help it, she broke out laughing. "We are, but it was just too good. I couldn't help myself." She looked at Cassie sheepishly through her laughter. "Sorry..."

"It's fine can we just get out of here, and to Jess's store? I'm really anxious to use these things." She shook the bag in her hand, which contained the pregnancy tests.

"Yeah, let's go get in the truck."

They went to Cassie's truck and Anna climbed in the driver's side. "You're going to have to give me directions Cassie. I'm not sure I'll be able to find this place without it."

"Sure, but, I don't think you'll need my help. It's kind of hard to miss."

Anna drove down the street a little farther.

God, she was right. Anna wouldn't have missed it if she was blinded and going the opposite direction. There was a giant stuffed bull out front of the store, and there was a stuffed deer, and a bear. Not to mention all the other animals.

"Seriously, Cass? I thought that this was an old timey store. Not the Walker, Montana taxidermist shop."

"Don't look at me I'm not the one who decided to do this with my store. That was Jess, talk to her."

Anna looked at Cassie like she was crazy for wanting to go there. "Okay, is this like a hobby of hers or something?"

Cassie just shook her head. "I guess you could say that. She goes hunting a lot. What else do you do with the animal once you've killed it?"

"I don't know get the meat and then dispose of the poor things body."

"Seriously, Anna? How have you survived living in the house? There are deer and elk heads everywhere."

Anna sighed and shook her head. "I don't know. That's different. It's not like their standing on the floor; their heads are attached to the walls. I don't mind the heads, but I just find the bodies standing on their own a little creepy."

Cassie started laughing so hard that she was holding her stomach while she convulsed in her seat with each laugh. "Oh, Anna you crack me up! Let's park and go in. I haven't seen Jess in a couple of weeks."

They found a spot quickly, and before they got out Cassie snagged the bag with the tests.

"What are you going to tell her when we go in?"

Cassie looked at Anna like she wasn't sure how to answer her. "I don't know...the truth."

That seemed to be enough of an answer for Anna because she didn't say anything in return. As they entered Anna seemed to be side stepping all the stuffed animals. It was so amusing that Cassie almost started laughing again.

Once they entered the store Anna was immediately in love. It was kind of a country home store. There was some old and new stuff. Part of the store was dedicated solely to clothing, and it was like the rest of the store, with some of it being new and old fashion styles.

When Jess saw Cassie he face lit up and she sashayed towards them. "Hey, I haven't seen you in a while. How have you been?"

Cassie shrugged her shoulders. "I've been okay. It's still hard you know, with Clint gone."

"I know I'm sorry, and who's this?" She asked motioning towards Anna as she flipped her dark blonde hair over her shoulder.

"That's Anna, my brother's girlfriend." She looked at Anna. "This is Jess."

"Hi it's nice to meet you. I'm glad to know that someone's finally trying to tame Brent."

"What? How many girls have tried to tame him?" Anna asked suspiciously.

Jess looked at her as if she was shocked that she didn't know. "Brent's quite popular in this town. Just about every girl has tried to tame him and make him their own, that is until you came about and did it in a matter of minutes."

"Oh." Anna said, looking extremely uncomfortable with the conversation that was going on.

Jess took the hint and changed the subject. "So Cassie, what's in the bag? Is it something for me?"

"Uh, no... Can we talk to you somewhere private?" Cassie looked around, hoping that no one was listening to the conversation that they were having.

"Sure, I'll just have my manager watch the store for a little while." Jess looked around until she spotted a red headed girl. "Hey, Maggie can you watch the store for me? It'll only be for a little while."

"Sure, boss." Maggie smiled at them.

"Thanks, just call me if you need me for anything. I'll be in the back." Jess told the girl, she couldn't be much older than twenty or twenty-one.

Jess directed them into the back of the store, which thank goodness was empty. "Okay, what's in the bag, and why are you being so secretive?"

Cassie set the bag on the table next to her and opened it up and then she grabbed the pregnancy tests out.

"What...?"

"Yup. That was my pretty much my reaction, Jess." Anna smiled at her.

Jess looked over at Cassie. "You're pregnant with Clint's baby."

Cassie nodded her head. "Well, I'm think I am, but I'm taking the tests just to be extra sure."

"Oh my, my, my. What have you gotten yourself into this time, Cass?" Jess asked her.

"Most likely life as a single mother..."

Jess and Anna each picked up a pregnancy test, and opened up their packaging. Anna was the first one to hand Cassie a test.

"Get in there and do whatever it is you have to do." Anna pointed towards the bathroom in the far left corner of the room.

Cassie walked over to the bathroom, repeatedly hitting her hand with the pregnancy test. She was nervous, she had an idea of what she was going to find out, but she wasn't sure what the results would be.

Anna and Jess waited outside of the bathroom talking quietly while they waited for Cassie to emerge with the tests results.

About fifteen minutes later Cassie exited the bathroom with the pregnancy test wrapped in a paper towel. "Hey, Anna," Anna whipped her head around to look at Cassie. "What does it say the sign on the test for being pregnant is?"

Anna grabbed the box and read the back of it. "The box says, two pink lines for being pregnant, and one for not being pregnant."

Cassie walked over to them and moved the paper towel to the side. In the middle of the test there were two pink lines staring the three of them square in the face.

"Oh my, God." Cassie dropped the test and you could hear it clank when it hit the hard wood floor.

"Wow..." Anna and Jess said simultaneously.

Jess looked at Cassie. "Here take the other one just so that were sure." Jess handed the second test over to Cassie.

Anna and Jess sat in silence for another fifteen minutes, while they waited for Cassie. They were both too nervous and excited to say a word.

The door to the bathroom opened once more and Cassie emerged with the other test wrapped in a paper towel.

"What does this one say?" Jess asked.

Cassie moved the paper towel away. "I'm not sure. The symbols on it are different than the ones on the other one. It looks like it's a pink line with a blue line going through the middle of it." Cassie picked up the box and looked at it. "It says that the sign says that I'm not pregnant." Her face fell, and a single tear trickled down her cheek. She'd been hoping for a mini Clint.

The other two got really close to Cassie and read the box, and then they looked at the test. They each saw the same thing that Cassie had. The test was negative.

"Anna is this the good pregnancy test or the cheap one that we got." Cassie asked her, trying not let anymore tears trickle from her eyes.

Anna grabbed the receipt from the bag and looked over it. "It's the cheap one."

Jess looked at Cassie, and she saw that more tears had fathen down her face. "Okay this means that it might not have been accurate. Maybe we should leave here and go to you OBGYN and have her do a blood test, or something. 'Cause you know blood doesn't lie."

"Yeah... I guess you're...right." She hiccupped as she spoke. "That's...what Anna suggested...we do next anyways." She continued to stare at the test in her hands, like it had taken away the last thing that she'd had, as she hiccupped.

Anna crossed over to her, and lifted her chin up so that they were looking eye to eye at each other. "It'll be okay. I know you want this baby, and for what you've told me it seems like you are pregnant. But if you don't end up being pregnant, you'll be fine. You may have to pull yourself up again like you had to when Clint left, but you'll be fine. You're a Donovan, so that just makes you extra strong. Okay?"

"Okay, then let's get going to my doctor's office, it's almost two o'clock." She wiped her face free of tears with her hands.

"Give me one second and I'll grab my purse, and then we can all go togeth-er." Jess crossed to an office in one of the corners and then she unlocked the door and grabbed her purse quickly before she close the door and locked it. "Let's go."

Anna picked up her purse and they all left the backroom together.

"Hey, Maggie, you're in charge. I should be back in an hour or two. If you need me call me, and I'll get back here as quickly as I can."

Maggie nodded at Jess, and the three of them headed towards the front door.

"You might want to call your doctor, Cass, and make sure that they know you're coming." Anna advised as the exited out into Main Street.

"I'll do that once we get in the truck." Cassie said as they walked towards the parking lot.

"Well, well, if it isn't Cassie Donovan. I haven't seen in a while. What's it been a year, two, more? Who really cares? How's Brent? Oh, God I can't wait to see him. You know he's the best I've ever had, and the stuff he bought me wasn't, too bad either. I'm sure he'll be glad to see me." Cassie turned around to find Leslie standing there.

All five foot six of her, with her long curly blonde hair and her light blue eyes. The nerve she had to comeback, wearing the Stetson hat and belt buckle Brent had bought her, no less. Cassie couldn't stand the woman.

Anna stared at her. So this was the woman that had hurt Brent so bad. Anna wanted to make her feel pain. She already felt jealous around her because of her past with Brent, but she'd be damned if she was going to let her take Brent away from her.

"Ah, if it isn't Leslie the slut. Why are you back here? I thought you were told not to come back." Cassie had Anna and Jess behind her for back up.

"You guys did, but I saw Brent's ad in that magazine and I decided that he needed me here. After all I was going to be his wife, why can't I just reclaim my position? Oh," she giggled evilly. "That's right I can. Hahah."

"He doesn't want you here Leslie. He's found someone knew, and there close to being engaged." Cassie glared at her enough to make Anna and Jess afraid of Cassie's wrath.

"I beg to differ Cassie, he called me the other day and he told me he wanted me back." Leslie smiled at her so confidently that her fakeness came through.

*****

You all probably hate me right now... Is Cassie really pregnant? I don' know, I guess you'll just have to wait for the next chapter to find out... Leslie's back, I'm sure you all want you claw my eyes out just for that little plot twist. Don't worry I hate her, too and I'm the one that created her. How could Brent do that to Anna? I don't know I guess have to wait for the next chapter to find out...

Okay, enough torturing you guys. Anyways, the next chapter should be up Saturday. The song on this side is a good one, I think it describes this chapter pretty well, Love Don't Live Here Anymore by Lady Antebellum.

Thanks for reading!!! Please comment and vote!!!

Chapter 16

C hapter 16

"What the f*ck did you just say Leslie?" Cassie questioned her.

"You heard me. Your brother wants me back. He said he's tired of the bimbo he's with." Leslie smiled demurely at them.

Anna stepped forward. "Excuse me; just who do you think you are? You think that you can just call me a bimbo and get away with it?!" Anna was fuming.

"I do. You can't even measure up to me you little slut. You have plain brown hair with split ends as far as the eye can see. Me, well, I'm blonde and blue eyed you can't get much better than that. Plus, you could stand to lose a couple of pounds." Jess and Cassie both looked ready to claw Leslie's eyes out. They gasped not believing what she'd said. "As for me I'm perfect you much have seen my picture in magazines and what not. You can't be fat if you want your photos to be plastered everywhere."

"You little b*tch. I can't believe you went there. And just so you know my name is Anna you dumb bimbo. Brent would never go with you. He's told me time and time again that he hates you, and wishes you the worst that can come to a person."

"Well, slutty Anna that's not what he said in the message that he left me on my phone." She said in a sing song voice.

"Okay you dumb b*tch you need to stop talking because you just sound like an unintelligent oversized b*tch. Got it slutty, bitchy Leslie? Brent is with me and he will never go for you again. He learned his lesson the first time. Wish for a second chance all you want, but you won't get one." Anna was ready to attack. This little bitch was going to try and take her man. Well, you know what she wasn't going to let that happen.

"Fine you don't believe me." She grabbed out her new Samsung S4 smart phone. Not shocking in the least, she probably got one of her new beaus to buy it for her. "Then how about you listen to the message you little sluts?"

Leslie messed with her phone a little bit and then all the sudden the voice mail was playing, and they all could hear Brent's voice. "Hey, babe it's me. I miss you. When are you coming home? Call me when you get this, it's been so long since I've last seen you, and I want you back. Talk to you later."

Anna stood there with her mouth wide open in shock. "No, no, it can't be true he... he wants me, not you."

"Obviously not. Now if you three will move, I have to buy an outfit for when I go and see Brent. Have fun with your hopeless love life slutty Anna. Oh, I really like that name for you." She cackled at Anna. "See y'all, next time you see me I'll have Brent's ring on my finger, again." She strutted away laughing at the three of them just standing there staring after her.

Anna hauled @ss the rest of the way back to the truck. She couldn't, wouldn't let anyone see the tears of hurt that Brent and Leslie had caused to spill from her eyes. She ended up sitting up against one of the truck tires.

How could he have done this to her?!

All he'd done was told her lies. She'd thought she could take his word and know that it was true, but now…

Now she didn't know anymore. It was like she was stuck in one of her romance novels or one of the ones she'd read. But this, this seemed so real, not like a book.

Real… Her life was seriously one-hundred percent, finally falling apart and it was like she was watching it all flash before her eyes.

Oh God, now she was going to have to go back to New York. Oh, how she loathed New York and everything about it except Chrissie.

Chrissie! How she missed her. Maybe moving back wouldn't be so bad as long as she always had Chrissie with her. Her loyal best friend through thick and thin and through hell and high water Chrissie would always be there for her.

"Anna?" Cassie asked hesitantly. "I'm sorry about what my brother did to you. I'm sorry about Leslie too, even though I can't control her."

Anna finally looked up, and tried to stop wallowing in her own self-pity. She wiped her eyes free of tears, embarrassed that she'd been crying against a truck in the middle parking lot while it was still the middle of the afternoon.

"It's okay." She croaked. "I think that I'll be okay, maybe once my heart heals from the break going down the middle of it. Although, that may not happen for ten or twenty years."

"Oh, Anna I know it hurts really badly, this is what I went through with Clint." Cassie helped Anna up from sitting position against the truck. "I can't believe he did this to you. I'm so, so sorry."

With a quick flick of her hands against her jeans Anna removed all the dirt from her hands. "Cass, I really don't want to think about this right now, or else I might crawl into a ball and start sobbing hysterically.

Cassie looked taken aback, Anna didn't want to talk about her lying, cheating, @sshole of a brother? "Okay, I guess..."

Jess finally spoke. "Why don't we all continue on to Cassie's doctor and then after were finished there we can go and find Brent and attack him for being a lying, cheating freaking scumbag? Sound good?"

*****

The sound of truck tires on a dirt road brought him out of his haze. Where Cass and Anna finally home? They'd been gone since God knows when and it was now almost four in the afternoon. What could have been so important that they'd had to make an impromptu trip into town for?

He didn't know. Brent had tried to understand the female brain, but unfortunately he was still completely rusty on the subject, and probably would be for the rest of his life. Females were a mystery to his male mind.

After putting up Mav's tack up Brent went outside of the barn to see if Cassie and Anna were home.

Ah, Anna, Brent honestly couldn't imagine a life without her anymore. She'd wrapped him around her finger, unknowingly and he found that he kind of liked it to be honest.

When Brent stepped out of the barn, he did not expect to find what he did.

Leslie Garrison, the woman that had made his life a living hell.

"Hey, cowboy. I bet you missed me." She smiled at him seductively.

Brent probably looked like someone had punched him in the stomach, and he felt like it, too, but he managed to regain his composure rather quickly. "No, Leslie. I honestly can't say that I have."

"Oh, poo, poo. You and I both know that's not true." She winked at him, and he just continued to stare at her.

"Well, believe it because it's very much the truth, and I don't like being questioned on what I say."

"You don't mean that. You're just trying to hurt me because I hurt you," She pouted and moved her blonde hair from her face.

"I'm sure you'll live." Brent grimaced he didn't know how one could be like her and manage to live with themselves. "Now get off my property. I told you a long time ago not to comeback. I'll forget this ever happened if you leave. If not fine by me, but then I'll be forced to take each measures in getting rid of you."

"But Brent, I've come to reclaim my position as your fiancée. Now you can kick that damn floozy Anna, back of to wherever she came from." She stepped a little closer to Brent and he retreated backwards a couple steps trying to get away from her.

"How the hell do you know about Anna?!" He questioned her. He was starting to get pissed off. He wanted Leslie gone, and he wanted her gone now.

"I met her in town earlier with your sister and a friend of hers. Don't worry I forgive you for dating other woman during my absence. Lord knows I wasn't a saint myself."

"You are about the farthest thing from a saint. The only words that really befit you are: cheating whore."

Leslie laughed shrilly. "Oh, you always did have a good sense of humor." Her face turned stone cold. "Now you listen to me. I am going to be your wife, and there is nothing you can do about it. Not unless you want me to ruin you. I can be very, and I mean very persuasive when I want to be." She played with a lock of her blonde hair, while her brown eyes bore holes into his.

"Not gonna happen. I have someone else know, and I want you to leave, or else I will be forced to call Sherriff Andrews out here, and you and I both know that he never liked you one bit." He smiled, Leslie had always been afraid of the Sherriff. "I'm sure he'd be glad to take out the trash for me."

"Seriously threatening me with Sherriff Andrews? Is that all you can come up with? I thought you were better than that."

Brent was barely keeping his anger in check. "Well, Leslie my mamma always told me men don't hit woman. And I am trying very hard not to throw that all out the window and smack you so hard that your gums bleed."

"So you like it rough now. Well that's fine by me."

He was getting so pissed off by her little playing dumb act. "Oh, you wish. Why don't you go find another hand and run off with him?"

"Because silly I want you, and your money."

This time it was Brent's turn to laugh. "So the truth finally comes out. I was wondering how long it was going to take for you to mention my money."

"You didn't seriously think that all the women in town fell for you because of your good looks, did you? No, Brent they want your money and that's it."

"That's nice. I have someone who's not fazed by my money and I am happy with her so now if you don't mind I'm going to go and call the sheriff and have you removed from my property. Don't be surprised if you get a restraining order in the mail." Brent started to walk towards the house for his phone.

"Anna's leaving you, you know."

That got his attention so fast that he whipped around and created a little plume of dust. "What did you just say?" He asked not so kindly.

Leslie shrugged at him. "Well, I made a mash up of voicemail that you'd sent me in the past, and now she believes that the reason I'm hear is because you called me and asked for me to come back so that we could be together." She smiled wickedly at him. "I'm sure she's making plans to leave your @ss and go back home to wherever she came from."

Brent was ragging mad now. "You little slut! How dare you think that you have a hold on my life, and that you can just waltz on in and destroy it for your own sick pleasure! Anna is the only woman I want." They could hear another truck coming up the road now. "You better fix this mess or else you will live an extremely miserable life from now on. Do you hear me?!"

She mock saluted him while she kept her bored looking stature. "Yes, sir, but I'm afraid I'm not going to take it back. I kind of like being the only woman in your life now."

"God dammit!!!" He bellowed.

The sound of a truck turning of and the sound of doors opening could be heard. Leslie looked around and saw that Anna, Cassie, and Jess were finally back.

Knowing that all eyes were on the two for them Leslie grabbed Brent by the shirt collar, and dragged her mouth against his. She wanted there to be no doubt in Anna's mind that Brent had now chosen her. Leslie sighed and moaned as loud as she could and make it sound real. Brent just stood there stunned by what Leslie was doing.

"What?! No, no, no, no, no, no! I can't believe this!" Brent heard Anna yell as she ran for the house after seeing them locked together.

Brent finally broke free of Leslie, and saw Anna run into the house, and then all he heard was the deafening sound of the front door being slammed.

"That's it Leslie! I'm calling the sheriff and having you removed now! Are you happy! You just ruined my one last shot at love! God f*cking dammit!!!" Brent stormed off past her in search for Anna.

*****

"Cassie, all of the pregnancy tests we did on you are coming up positive. It looks like you are going to be a mother." Her doctor said as she smiled at her.

A mini Clint!

She'd never been so happy in her life. It was official she was going to be a mommy.

"From what I've found, your due date will be June17th. Congratulations!"

"Thank you, doctor." Cassie picked up her purse.

"I think were finished here. On your way out go and see my secretary out in the lobby, and she will get your first ultrasound appointment set up. You should find out the sex of the baby then." The doctor moved a lock of light brown hair out of her face, and led Cassie, Jess, and Anna out into the lobby. "Have a nice day. I'll see you soon."

"Thank you again, doctor."

Once Cassie had set up her next appointment Anna went up and stood next to her. "I told you everything would work out."

"Thanks Anna, for everything. I really mean it. Where would I be without you?"

Anna smiled a small smile at her. "I don't know, but I'm sure you'd be just fine."

"Maybe," Cassie smiled grimly at Anna. "I just hope everything works out for you. I'm just sorry this all happened to you."

Anna's face fell, until then she'd managed not to think about it for the past hour.

Jess picked up on Anna's mood change and decided to change the subject before it could go any farther. "How about we go back to the ranch, and boot the men – or man – out and have ourselves a girls night?"

Anna smiled at her. "Fine by me. I don't know if I can face Brent right now anyways."

On the way home they chatted out everything, well, except for the sore subject of Brent and what was going on there.

When they pulled up to the house all three of them saw Leslie and Brent talking about half way between the barn and the house. They all got out of the truck and then Leslie hauled Brent against her and they started to kiss.

Anna's world came crashing down the second she saw the kiss. So it was true. He didn't want her.

Anna's heart broke – no it shattered into a million pieces at her feet. "What?! No, no, no, no, no, no! I can't believe this!"

Anna ran into the house as hot tears began to run down her face. She heard Brent yelling in the distance, but she was too far gone anymore to care. She ran up the stairs and into her room and then she collapsed on her bed and began to sob hysterically.

So this is what it felt like to have your heart broken, she thought as she sobbed.

*****

So, how many of you hate me right now? Show of hands?

I'm sorry it's probably not the drama you wanted. Hey, at least you know that Brent's innocent. I hope that makes up for the unwanted drama.

The song on the side is She Won't Be Lonely Long by Clay Walker.

Also go and check out the synopsis for Cassie's story, Runaway Bride!!!

I hope you enjoyed the chapter!!! Please vote and comment!!! Thanks for reading!!!

Chapter 17

C hapter 17

"Cassie can you call Sheriff Andrews, I want Leslie gone now?" Brent asked his sister as he began to trudge his way towards the house.

"Fine, but you owe me big time. I don't take watching her very lightly." Cassie glared over Leslie's way.

"Okay, whatever. I owe you...big time. Just watch he until the sheriff gets here." He kicked his boots in the dirt. "I have to go and try to fix my relationship with Anna."

Brent continued walking towards the house.

Jess looked at Cassie. "How does he plan to fix this?"

Cassie shook her head. "You know, I'm kind of wondering the same thing. But for now we can at least help him by getting rid of her," she motioned towards Leslie.

"Want me to call the sheriff?" Jess asked Cassie curiously.

"Sure. Tell him to get out here quick. I don't want her on our land any longer than we have to."

"I'll go call him in just a minute, but first why don't you just let her leave with a warning?" Jess was confused, why should they get the sheriff in the middle of this?

"Well, because the last time he tried that it obviously didn't work. I mean she came back. Didn't she?"

Jess bit the corner of her mouth, a bad habit she'd acquired. "Yeah."

"Getting the law involved might make things seem a little more real to her...and then maybe she'll finally leave all of us alone."

"True. I'll go and call Sheriff Andrews. Have fun with Leslie while I'm gone." Jess walked over toward the barn to call the sheriff.

Cassie looked away from Jess walking off. "So what's your problem, Leslie? Why do you feel the need to destroy my brother's happiness?"

She got no response.

"Leslie, I don't know what to do with you anymore. We gave you the chance to just walk away. I don't want to get involved with the law, but honestly, I don't think we know another way to deal with you."

There was still no response.

Cassie was done. She couldn't think of any other way to deal with Leslie. So they'd get the sheriff over her, charge her with trespassing and verbal threat. This was the last that they'd ever see of her.

*****

"Anna?!" Brent knocked on her door. "Please talk to me... It's not what you think." He sighed loudly when no response came. "Please, I really need to talk to you. I don't want to lose you, Anna."

He could hear her sobbing on the other side of the door. He didn't know what to do. Should he go in and try and comfort her, help her understand his side? Or should he walk away and let her cool off?

So many questions, which one should he choose? All Brent knew is that he didn't want to lose her. He hadn't figured out his feelings for her, yet, but he did know that if he lost her might be akin dying. There was no life for him, at least not one that didn't include Anna.

He'd made his choice. He opened the door and found her curled up on her bed while silent tears poured out of her eyes.

His heart broke knowing that he'd been the one who caused those tears to fall from her eyes. Looking at her crying, made him feel like he'd been hit by a ten ton truck, or at least sucker punched in the stomach

"I'm so sorry...Anna. I didn't know that she was going to come here. If I would have known I would have scared her off before she could have gotten a chance to take this whole situation as far as she did." Anna still hadn't looked at him so he leaned against her wardrobe.

Anna moved her eyes up to look at him, but even that hurt. It hurt looking at the man she loved, knowing that he'd lied to her. Her heart was torn in two because she loved this man more than her life. She knew that her heart would never fully heal from his betrayal.

That kiss.

She wanted to cry and rip him limb from limb because of the kiss. He'd never know how much seeing that kiss hurt her.

Anna rolled over so that she wouldn't have to look at him. "How can I believe what you say anymore...?" Brent sighed, and sat down on the floor of the other side of the bed so that she would look at him. "I know you called her a little while ago."

Brent rubbed his hand over his face. "I never called her. I wouldn't do that to you, but I know that you probably don't believe me right now."

Not believe him. Of course she didn't believe him. She saw him kissing Leslie for God's sake.

Anna looked out her window and saw a storm coming. The first snow storm of the season, and it was going to be a one by the looks of the clouds, dark and gloomy just the way she was feeling.

"I can't believe you. There's no proof that you are innocent in all of this. Well, none that I've seen." She sighed and sat up in her bed to look at him, her back leaning against the headboard.

"Will you give me time to prove myself to you? I can't lose you, Anna." Brent didn't know what to do. Anna was pulling away from him, and all because of Leslie. He didn't know id he could survive losing her.

She looked at him stubbornly with tear streaks on her face. "I don't know. I won't, and I mean I won't let you hurt me again."

Brent closed his eyes and tried to stay calm. He didn't want to fight with her. "I didn't mean to hurt you. Does any of the stuff I told you about Leslie mean a damn thing? Huh. I told you that I was happy to be done with Leslie and her games." He paused for a minute gathering his thoughts. "Are you going to forget everything and believe her?"

"Maybe... You hurt me more than anyone has ever hurt me before. And you know that's hard to do especially after what my parents did to me." She could hardly stand too look at him. Every time she did, the break in her heart was more pronounced, and she could barely breathe from the pain it caused her.

"I don't want to fight with you I care about you too much for that. The only problem is that you won't believe anything I say, will you?" Anna nodded her head no. "That's what I thought."

"Will you please go away?" Anna didn't want to talk to him, the pain she was feeling from being near him was suffocating her, and making her angry.

"No, we need to talk this out. I don't want us to end."

Anna glared at him viciously. "There isn't an "us". Remember? You destroyed that possibility when you called Leslie. Don't tell me you didn't. You could have lied to me when you talked about her."

He snorted angrily. "Ohhh, that's rich you know? You know that I don't lie, Anna."

"Since when do I know that? You could have been lying to me all along." Anna felt more tears coming. She wanted to believe him, but it hurt so bad, trying to moving from the dark to the light.

"So does this mean that all those kisses, special moments we shared were fake, too?" Before she tried to speak again he continued on. "They weren't Anna. They mean more to me than all the stars combined."

She shook her head. "No, I don't believe you." She said quietly, a tear leaking out of the corner of her eye.

He knew she was trying not to believe him, trying to guard her heart from the pain she felt looming over her head. "Do you want me to kiss you again? Help you know that they weren't fake? Help you know that I meant every single one of them? Help you feel that spark, the intensity of it all making your toes curl because that's what I felt." He sighed and moved closer to her, but she quickly looking down hiding the emotions spreading across her face.

"Please, don't," she cried.

Brent grabbed her chin. "Please don't, what?" She shied away from his touch. "Hey, I'm not going to hurt you. I would never hurt you, the thought kills me inside." He whispered to her.

Anna was caught by surprise when she was looking into his eyes as his mouth lowered itself onto hers. She gasped, but finally gave into him. As much as she hated him right now she couldn't deny either of them the wonder of a kiss.

She felt her walls starting to fall down again. She wouldn't—couldn't let him in so easily. "No, please no." She pushed him away even though it probably hurt her more than it did him. "I can't do this—I won't do this. Get away from me." She yelled at him.

"Anna please don't push me away. Please, I'll do anything just don't push me away. Please," He begged her.

He was lying she kept telling herself. "No, I don't want to be near you. Go away! I can't do this anymore. I can't deal with you!"

"Come on. You don't have to do this. Hear me out. Okay."

"No! Now, go!" He stared at her, it was apparent to him that he had lost this argument.

"Fine! I'm not going to leave you alone forever. I'll give you one night and then were going to talk about all of this. You hear me? Good!" He stalked towards the door, and then slammed it on the way out.

*****

For some reason while they waited for the sheriff to arrive, Leslie felt guilt wash over her. She didn't know why she acted the way that she did. She just did...

Never in her life had she felt so awful about something she'd done. She destroyed a love match in a few short hours. She knew Brent loved Anna, he just didn't see it yet. She needed to fix everything; this wasn't who she wanted to be. If her dear old mom was looking down on her now, she knew that she'd be extremely disappointed in her.

"I'm sorry," she whispered as she was standing behind Cassie.

Cassie whipped around to look at her. "What did you say?"

Leslie looked up at her. "I'm so sorry."

To be honest Cassie wasn't sure what to make of her sudden change in heart. "Sorry for what? For destroying my brother? For destroying a kind woman that never did anything to you?"

"Yes, I honestly don't know why I did the things I did. I'm not going to take them back because I can't. None of the things I told you were true. Tell Anna that. Tell her I'm sorry for that kiss."

"Why are you trying to be sincere all of the sudden?"

"I don't know. I'll take whatever punishment you want me to."

Jess joined them again. "She's trying to apologize," Cassie told Jess.

"She is," Jess asked.

"Yes and you are going to be my witness, just in case she ever changes her mind, and comes back again."

"Fine with me," Jess changed the subject. "Sheriff Andrews said he'd be here in a few. He's at another ranch close to here so it should take him long to get here."

"Great! I'm not sure how much longer I want to listen to her trying to be sincere." Leslie just stood there and listened to them talk to each other.

"I can hear you, you know."

Cassie smiled. "We know."

"So you're going to leave them alone?" Jess asked Leslie.

"Yes…"

"Good they've worked too hard to get over dealing with you, to have to put up with you in their lives again." Jess looks over at Cassie. "They're done with you."

"I know they are. I don't blame them either."

A Dodge Charger pulled in next to Cassie's truck, and the sheriff stepped out. "How are you ladies?" he asked Cassie and Jess.

"Fine," they responded.

"And you must be the person I'm here to get." He looked over at Leslie then at Cassie with a smile on his face. "What'd she do?"

"Well, first of she trespassed onto land that she told she was not allowed on. Then she threatened to destroy my brother's life, and apparently she was extremely serious." Cassie told him and smiled at him.

"I can write her up for trespassing, and as for the threat I don't know if I'll be able to make anything stick, but I can check when I get back to the precinct. Do you want me to arrest her?"

Cassie looked at him and sighed. "No, but I wouldn't mind if you scared her a little, make sure she won't be bothering us anymore."

"Sure thing, Miss Donovan." He turned to Leslie. "I'm going to load you up into my squad car without the cuffs, but if you resist I will be forced to cuff you. Go it?"

Leslie just nodded, not saying a word. "I'll be seeing you ladies." He tipped his Stetson at Cassie and he smiled at her. "Miss Donovan." Then he tipped his Stetson at Jess with a smile. "Miss Evans."

He drove off with Leslie and Jess flipped her hair over her shoulder and said, "That man is dreamy, Cassie."

*****

Sorry about the wait for this chapter, but here it is. The song on the side is, Come Wake Me Up by Rascal Flatts. It's a fitting song for this chapter, especially Anna's state of mind.

I hope you enjoyed this chapter! Please vote and comment!

Chapter 18

C hapter 18

"Leslie lied to all of us." Cassie told Anna as she walked into her room. Anna was lying in a heap upon the bed with red puffy cheeks, and mated hair.

"She did?" She started to sit up on her bed.

"Yes, she confessed to the whole thing while we were waiting for Sherriff Andrews to come and get her." Cassie paused a second. "She wanted me to tell you that she was sorry."

Anna sat there and looked dumb. "She did?" She looked completely confused. "Are you shitting me?"

"No I'm really not. Jess and I think that she had a change of heart. We don't know why, but she did."

"So Brent's wasn't lying to me. It was all Leslie, and he really does care about me?" Her statement came out as more of a question than a statement.

"Yes, he really does."

Anna still looked confused as she sat there. "But he kissed her back," she kind of mumbled.

"So... Leslie can be a very convincing person. You saw what she wanted you to believe. My brother can be an asshole, but he would never cheat on a person."

"I don't know Cassie. I haven't known him as long as you have, only for a couple of months." She still looked unsure, but Cassie knew that she could come around and realize Brent wouldn't ever be a cheater.

"Well, I know my brother, and I know that he would never do that to you. Have you ever seen the way he looks at you?" Anna shook her head 'no'. "Well, I have. He looks at you like he couldn't live without you, like he'd die if you ever left him. To him, the sun rises and sets because of you."

Anna looked at her as if she wasn't quite sure if she believed her.

Cassie continued on. "Now I don't know if he loves you, but I do know that he's on his way there. He may realize it tomorrow, next week or, next month, but the think about love, Anna, is that it's worth waiting for." Cassie put a serious look on her face. "Now when he gets back here from wherever he's gone I want you guys to talk, and work things out. Got it?"

"Yeah, I do, but I'm still unsure about this whole thing, and how it will end?"

"You'll be fine, but how 'bout in the mean while we go and hang out with Jess in the living room, and have a girl's night." Cassie was holding open Anna's door.

"Sure," Anna got up and followed her out.

*****

Brent walked in the house that night with a little weight taken off of his shoulders. After his confrontation with Anna he'd gotten a call from one of the guys, telling him about how they were going to Middle Fork up in Hobson, Montana for a hunting trip.

He'd agreed knowing that he had to get away for a little while. He needed space from Anna, and she needed some away from him. This would be the first time they'd been apart, and maybe they could get over the things that had happened. Hopefully helping them to realize that they belonged together, and that nothing could or would ever change that.

In the morning they'd have to start figuring things out on their own because that's when he was leaving. Brent was going to miss her like crazy, but this was the only thing that he could think of to do, so that they could get their relationship back on track.

When he walk in the house he found two very—and he meant very—tipsy females, and one not so tipsy, but sleepy female, all watching the lifetime channel while they talked about their failures in the love department. Anna was smiling at something, and he almost couldn't tear his eyes away from her, even though he was mad at her for not believing him, she was still breath taking when she smiled.

The coffee table had at least two empty bottles of wine on it, no wonder why they were tipsy. "I think it's time for this little party to get shut down. It's almost eleven o'clock." He looked Cassie's way. "We need to talk, but first we have to get Jess set up in the guest room, some coffee into you to wake you up, and Anna in bed as well, and tall glasses of water, and an aspirin on Jess and Anna's night stands."

Brent quickly went upstairs and put fresh sheets on the bed that Jess would be sleeping on, and also to add a note to Anna's night stand telling her that he'd be gone for a couple of days, among other things.

When he got downstairs a couple of minutes later he found Anna passed out on the couch and jess sitting next to her while Cassie tried to make coffee in her sleepy state.

He tipped his head into the kitchen where Cassie was. "I'm going to carry Anna up to her bed."

Cassie looked at him, and her eyes started to flutter closed. "Sure, okay. We'll talk when you get back downstairs."

Brent left the kitchen and went back to Anna. She was still in the same position on the couch, she looked so peaceful, and he knew right then in that very moment that he'd never loved anyone more in his life, than he did Anna. He loved her because she was Anna, she wasn't perfect, but she was real and he found that completely refreshing.

Extremely carefully he picked up Anna up, and he held her in his arms much like a man would carry his bride over the threshold. She stirred a little, but for the most part stayed she stayed tucked in his arms. As Brent made his way up the stairs he was very careful, as to not wake her up.

When Brent opened up the door he cringed, and looked at Anna, but she hadn't stirred at all, which he was grateful for. He shifted Anna a little in his arms so that he could pull down the covers on her bed, and placed her on them. With a quick tug of the comforter he had her covered up in seconds. Anna stirred a little bit when she felt the fabric covering herself.

The urge to lie down next to her and hold her for the night was almost overwhelming, but he had to hold himself back.

He put his hand to her cheek and then he kissed her lips and then her forehead. "I love you, Anna." He'd always thought that it would be hard to say that to a woman, but honestly it was surprisingly easy. Brent kissed her once more on the forehead and then he left the room.

Once back down stairs he found that Jess had already gone upstairs to bed. Cassie was sitting at the island in the kitchen nursing a cup of black decaf coffee.

"Hey, sis." He opened up the cabinet above the coffee maker, and grabbed a mug. After filling it he took a seat next to Cassie.

"I'm going to be leaving in the morning." He told her.

"Leaving? Where are you going?" Cassie asked him while she drank a sip of decaf coffee.

"I'm going with a couple of the guys to Middle Fork on a hunting trip. I could be gone anywhere from a couple of days to a week. It all depends on how great the hunting is."

Cassie looked over at him. "Oh, okay. I know that Anna wants to talk to you. I told her that Leslie lied about everything, and she kind of believes me, but you still need to talk to her." She pushed the mug away from her, and crossed her arms.

"I'll talk to her once I get back. This will give us both a chance to think about our relationship, and where we want it to go. I'll miss her like crazy, but it won't be for long, and like I said we both need the time away from each other."

Cassie looked at him expectantly. "Are you in love with her? Are you in love with, Anna?" She questioned him.

He shifted uncomfortably on his stool, not knowing exactly what to say. "I do, more than I've ever loved anyone in my whole life."

Cassie immediately perked up. "You do! Are you going to marry her! Oh my gosh! Have you told her yet!?"

"Not really, when I put her in her bed tonight I told her, but I highly doubt that she heard me." He shook his head at Cassie. "Now I don't want you to tell her, or anyone else for that matter. I know how you can be."

"I won't. Oh my goodness this is such good news! But you never answered me when I asked you if you are going to marry her."

"I'm sure I will—someday—if I have any say, but I don't know what Anna's feelings about the possibility of marrying me are." He took a big gulp of coffee from his mug.

"She loves you, too. Don't ask me how I know, but you have to tell her when she is awake." Cassie stood up and did a happy dance. "I'm going to have a sister."

"Calm down, nothings official yet." He sighed and shook his head at his sister.

She put a hand to her stomach. "Sorry, I just can't help it. I've always wanted a sister."

Brent was completely oblivious of the way she put her hand to her stomach. "What am I? Chopped liver?"

"No," she sighed, "but let's face it you're not a girl."

"Okay, sure. I think I'm going to go to bed now. I have to be ready to leave in a few hours."

"Do you have everything packed?" she asked him.

"Most of it, I just have to put my clothes, and toiletries into a suit case, and then I'll be ready to go. I should be able to get my bag packed in about fifteen minutes, and the truck is filled with everything else we'll need. I'll say bye to you in the morning before I leave." He told her as he got up, and put his now empty mug into the sink.

She yawned. "Okay, see you in the morning." She left the kitchen for upstairs, and he followed her.

Instead of going to his own room, he made his way to Anna's. He couldn't explain why, but he wanted to hold Anna tonight while she was in a deep sleep, and wouldn't be able reprimand him.

When he opened the door he saw that she was sprawled out on the bed, clutching the comforter to her chest. He pulled off his boots, and pulled down the covers on the other side of her bed. When he lied down next to her she stirred, but never woke up. He pulled her to his chest, and swore that no one, but Anna would ever feel right lying in his arms.

Brent found himself quickly drifting off.

The next morning when he woke up, Anna's face was pressed up against his chest and she was drooling on his shirt while she snored. She looked absolutely adorable to him.

One glance at her alarm clock told him that it was almost five, and he had to meet the guys in town at seven. Brent nuzzled his nose down into Anna's neck, and sighed, he could give himself five more minutes lying next to her. Next he moved his nose to her hair. It smelled just like honeysuckle mixed with vanilla. He loved that smell.

He could most definitely get used to lazy mornings holding Anna. He'd have to win her over first. Somehow they would get past Leslie's lies.

Brent stretched out, and let out a yawn. When he stretched Anna stirred a little bit, but still remained asleep. That was when he made his getaway. He got up from the bed and made his way to the nightstand on her side of the bed.

The note he'd placed on the night stand the night before was still sitting there. Brent quickly found and pen and opened it up. At the bottom it said, Brent. He quickly scribbled above that, Love.

He wanted so bad to wake her up, and kiss her, and tell her that he loved her while she was coherent. Instead he settled to kiss her on her forehead. He fluffed the pillow his head had laid on, and smoothed out the comforter on the side of the bed he'd slept on. It was almost like he'd never been there at all.

*****

That morning—more like afternoon—when Anna woke up she stretched. She'd had the most delicious dream. Brent had held her, and slept next to her in her bed. It had been the best dream that she's ever had in her life. Even though she was uncertain about their relationship, she couldn't help, but revel in how great it would be to be held all night long by the man she loved.

She looked to the side of her, and she found a glass of water, and aspirin, and a note on her bedside table. There was dull ache in her head so she snatched the aspirin, and then swallowed it down with the water. Next she grabbed the note, and opened it.

Anna,

I know that you may not want to talk to me after everything that has happened. I just want you to know that I'm sorry, and that I would never do anything to intentionally hurt you. I just hope that you will come to believe me soon.

In the morning when you wake up I will be gone. Don't worry about me. I've left on a hunting trip with a couple of the guys to Middle Fork, which is up in Hobson, Montana. I shouldn't be gone any more than a week.

My trip will be good for us. It'll give us time to think about what we want, and where our priorities stand. I want you to know that I don't want you to leave, but if by the time I'm home you're gone... Well, then I guess I'll have to deal with that but, please, please don't leave me.

Love,

Brent

*****

Sorry this took so long. I kept getting writers block. I think it's because this is the first story that I will have finished, and I don't want it to. I want to keep writing this story, but as they say, all good things have to come to an and. Right?

On Friday, July 5th it will be one year since I have joined Wattpad. How exciting!!!

The song on the side is, She's Everything by Brad Paisley. I think it fits how Brent feels about Anna. Give it a listen. Also, please comment and vote! I hope you enjoyed the chapter!!!

Chapter 19

C hapter 19

"Hey, sleepy head." Cassie said when Anna walked into the kitchen a little after noon clutching something in her hand. Cassie was sitting at the island holding a cup of decaf coffee, and while she read a book.

"Hey. Did Brent really leave?" Anna asked as she grabbed a mug from the cabinet above the coffee maker.

"Yeah, it was sometime around six or seven I think." Cassie set her book off to the side, and motioned towards the coffee maker. "There's regular coffee in there, and decaf on the stove in the percolator."

"Thanks." Anna yawned, covering her mouth with the hand that was not holding the mug. "I had the sweetest dream last night."

Cassie smiled to herself; she had a pretty good idea of what they were about. "That can happen to a person when they're drunk. What were they about?"

There was a small smile on Anna's face as she filled her mug with the steaming hot coffee. "You brother held me all night long while we slept, it was really sweet."

"I hate to burst your bubble, but that wasn't a dream." Anna was so shocked by Cassie's revelation that she almost dropped her mug.

"What do you mean it wasn't a dream?" She was starting to feel a bit uncomfortable.

"Last night when I came upstairs to go to bed, I decided that I'd check on you and Jess to make sure you were both alright. When I opened your door I found you Brent holding you, and you were both completely contempt, and sound asleep. Jess is still zonked out upstairs, just in case you were wondering."

The kitchen was silent for a minute. "Oh... I guess that explains why I got the best night of sleep I've ever had. I must have been really comfortable."

"Yeah, you two sure looked cozy." She changed the subject. "Did Brent leave you a note?"

"He did," Anna quickly set down her mug on the island, and opened the piece of paper she'd had in her hand, and then handed it Cassie.

"Have you thought any more about your guys' relationship?" Cassie questioned her as she handed the note back.

"A little," Anna said, as she opened the fridge and grabbed the bacon, eggs, and bread. "Do you want some breakfast, or should I say brunch since it's almost noon?"

"Sure, do you want some help?" Cassie got up from her chair, and went and grabbed a couple of pans for the bacon and eggs to cook in.

"That would be great," Anna said, as she set all the food down next to the stove.

Together they cooked the meal in silence. It took about fifteen minutes for everything to cook, and by then Jess was finally awake and sitting at the island.

"Good afternoon, sleepy head." Cassie told her as she set a plate of food in front of Jess, and then sat next to Jess with her own plate. Next, Anna followed suit, and sat on the other side of Jess.

"How much wine did I have last night," Jess asked as she put her head in her hands and sighed. The brightness of the light was killing her. The aspirin, and glass of water helped, but not enough.

"I'd say a little over a bottle," Anna told her, as she ate a bite of her eggs. "I think you had about three glasses of wine, I know that I only had two."

"That would explain it. I've never been able to stand my own when it comes to wine."

"Wine makes me sleepy." Anna said as she yawned.

"Could you two stop bragging about drinking?" Cassie pouted. "I can't have any for another two, or three years."

Jess and Anna both just laughed. "Stop winning, you're the one who did the horizontal tango," Jess spoke up.

"Okay, ha, ha. You guys can have the last laugh," She laughed at them. "I'm going to go and take a shower." Cassie snatched her bacon up and left the table.

*****

Middle Fork was always stunning in the winter time. Brent wished Anna was there to see it with him. Maybe this time next year they'd be married, and could come up for a short vacation. Although, with the way he was feeling about her, they probably wouldn't make it farther than the bed in their hotel room, or tent if they decided to stay in one.

There he went again, getting ahead of himself. He didn't even know if Anna would still be there when he got home or if she was going to end things when he got back. He hoped, and prayed not, but their fate wasn't in his hands anymore.

"What's got you so distracted, Brent?" One of the guys, James asked.

"Nothin' that some good huntin' can't fix." All the guys erupted in laughter.

"Here, here to that!" They all cheered as they took sips of their beers. They were at the bar in town having a little kick-off to their trip. Tomorrow they'd kill some deer and elk, but tonight they were going to get a little rowdy, drink a little too much.

Two beers later Brent, was tired of the bar scene. He paid his tab, and walk out into the crisp winter night. It was a little before seven thirty, so he knew that most of the shops in town were still open.

At the end of the street there was a sign that said, "Jane's Jewels". Brent had nothing else to do so he walked over to the shop. In the window there was an engagement ring, and he couldn't take his eyes off of it. It had a horseshoe smack dab in the middle, shaped with multiple different diamonds, and there were small diamonds going around the band.

It was Anna in a ring. The horseshoe represented her love for horse, nature, along with ranch life. And the diamonds were the brightness that she brought into everyone that knew hers life.

He had to buy that ring for her. It was the perfect thing to show her that he knew her, and that he loved her.

The sign in the window said that they closed at eight, so he had to go inside right then, and get that ring. No other one would do.

The bell on the door chimed and he waked inside. There was a woman in her early forties standing at the counter reading a country living magazine, and she looked up when she heard the bell chime. "May I help you?" She asked him as she looked him over.

"Um, yes. There's a ring in the window that I'm interested in." he told her, and she guided him over to the window.

"Which one is it?" Brent pointed at the horseshoe ring. "Great choice. That ring is one of a kind. I'm guessing very much so like the one it's intended for."

Brent nodded his head in agreement. "It is. I wanted to look at it... and possibly buy it."

The saleswoman laughed at him. "Nervous are we? Okay." She grabbed the ring from its pedestal, and took it over to the counter. "This ring is about three carats, the diamonds are princess cut, and the medal is white gold."

"How much is it?" Brent asked her as her studied the ring in her hand.

"Are you sure you want to know?" She asked him curiously. "Never mind of course you do. With its cut, design, and size of diamonds it's about twelve thousand dollars."

Brent gasped. Twelve thousand dollars! He had enough money to buy it and then be able to pay for a one hundred thousand dollar wedding, but still, twelve thousand dollars for a ring?!

But it was the perfect ring, the only ring he could imagine to be place on Anna's finger, his ring, the ring that he chose for her. Nothing else would do.

"I'll take it. Could your ring it up while I approve the purchase with my credit card company?" the lady nodded, and Brent slipped outside quickly.

A few short minutes later he entered the store again, and handed the woman his credit card. She typed a couple things on her register, and then hand the card back to him.

"This ring has a lifetime warranty," she told him. "You'll need to call the number on the back of your receipt if you ever need to have anything fixed or replaced on it." She put the ring in a nice little bag that had the name of the store printed onto it. "Also, since this ring is one of a kind it's a size ten so that if it's too big you can have it resized."

"Thank you."

"You are very welcome. I hope you have a happy life with your lady."

Brent full out grinned. "Thank you! I plan to." He exited the shop, and walked to his hotel thinking about the future he would have with Anna.

*****

It'd been three days since Brent had left, and no one had heard a word from him. And during those days Anna had felt an ache so strong in her chest that she could barely breathe without the pain of missing Brent.

She felt guilty about not talking to him after she yelled at him in her room. The last time she'd seen him while she was awake was when his walked into the house, and found her a little tipsy in the living room with Cassie and Jess.

She knew he'd held her during the night, and honestly she couldn't imagine going to bed without him anymore, even though she'd been alone the past couple of nights.

Anna was coming to realize that love was hard, and made you feel like you wanted to crawl into a ball and die when you were without the one you loved.

Over the past couple days Anna had come to forgive Brent. They'd all been played by Leslie. He couldn't help that Leslie had wanted to destroy everything. All Anna could do was to try and apologize for ever doubting him.

The storm that had been coming seemed like it had been getting worse since Brent's departure, and Anna just hoped he was staying safe and away from the blizzard as much as he possibly could.

Although, they weren't talking, yet she didn't—and would never—wish him any harm. She loved the stubborn crazy man more than anyone else in the whole world. The only problem with that was when would she tell him, and how would she do it. She had her reservations about if he loved her yet, or if he was still in the liking a lot phase of the relationship.

If he was then Anna knew she'd be a little bummed. She wanted him to love her as much as she loved him.

Love was a crazy thing, Anna though. It could make you fill giddy inside. Break your heart into a million pieces. And when you were lucky you could fine the, real never ending true love.

The kind that Anna knew she had found with Brent. The kind where it hurt to be away from the one you loved for even a minute. The kind of love that could tear you apart inside if it ever ended. The kind where one kiss or touch could set your blood ablaze, and make you weak at your knees.

"What are you thinking about?" Cassie asked when she saw Anna standing in front of the bay window in the living room.

Anna slowly turned around. "Your brother..." she let the thought trail off.

"Okay, what about him?"

Anna fidgeted with her hands. "I'm worried about him, Cassie, you and I know that when he has a lot on his mind he can do stupid things. I just hope he doesn't do anything stupid while he's out hunting in this storm." Her eyes filled with a few tears, and her faced looked tired and a bit worried.

"Hey, it's okay. He'll be fine." Cassie hugged her, trying to soothe Anna's worries.

The tears Anna had been trying to hold in betrayed her as they flowed down her face. "But we don't know that. Cassie this storm is making it frigid, along all the snow we're getting. I just don't want anything to happen without him knowing that I love him, and that I've forgiven him." Sobs slowly racked Anna's body.

Cassie quickly realized that Anna was just about as inconsolable as anyone could get. And if Cassie was be true to herself, she too was worried about Brent. This storm had the possibility of dropping the temp to below zero, and they had the possibility of get multiple feet of thick, heavy snow.

Cassie rubbed soothing circles along Anna's back. "Shhh, everything will be fine."

"How-how can y-you know that," Anna whimpered.

"I don't, but I'm hopeful that everything will be fine. That's what we have to do. Hope for the best, and prepare for the worst. Brent's smart he'll be fine."

Anna tried to calm herself, freaking out would do nothing, but make her scared about Brent's safety. Why could he just have gone later when there was no storming lurching over them?

If he hadn't then he wouldn't be the crazy, stubborn man Anna had fallen for.

Oh, God. It was her fault that he was gone. If they hadn't have fought then he would never have left on that if damn trip.

"It's all my fault. If we hadn't of fought he wouldn't have felt the need to leave, so that we could cool off." Anna felt awful, she thought she might be sick.

She was a monster. She should have listened to him instead of being so God damn stubborn. Curse her stubborn soul.

"It's not your fault Anna. He would have gone anyways. It's hunting season. No man can resist—or should I say real man—can resist shooting things, and letting their testosterone run wild." Cassie laughed at her joke, and Anna let a small smile grace her lips.

Anna wasn't so sure about it not being her fault, but she could try and give herself the benefit of the doubt.

"Come on, I have fresh chocolate chip cookies, and hot chocolate on the stove. Let's go eat and drink it all so we don't feel awful about anything." Cassie sais as she led the way to the kitchen.

"I kind of like your cravings Cassie, but I have a feeling I'm going to get fat from them." Anna tried to be carefree—even though she was nowhere close to that—and joke a little with Cassie.

"You?! What about me?! I'm going to be the size of a whale from all these cravings!" Cassie squealed.

*****

My trip to the University of Wyoming went so well. I talked to the Army ROTC people, and it looks like I will be joining the Wyoming National Guard some time this year, or next year. That way I'll get in state tuition, and they basically pay for everything, but about three-fourths of my room and board. I also was told that I'm practically admitted, and that I have been accepted into the pre-nursing program, so no worries there. I guess we all know where I'm going to college next year after I graduate from high school.

Thank you all for being so patient! I've been so busy this past week with my trip, and starting to get my fitness levels to where they need to be.

Anyways, a big storm is coming. I wonder what's going to happen...? Aren't you so happy that Anna has finally stopped being so pigheaded, but I feel kind of bad for her. She thinks the whole thing is her fault. Poor Anna.

The song on the side is absolutely perfect for Anna and Brent. It's You Make It Look So Easy by Eric Church. I love Eric Church... Then again who doesn't?

Thanks for reading!!! Please comment and vote!

Chapter 20

C hapter 20

"I think it's time for us to leave. The snow is going to be starting to come in pretty heavy. We might just want to pack up, and leave for home tonight. I mean we have plenty of fresh meat to last us all until next season." One of the guys suggested.

"You guys head on to the hotel. I'll be back in a couple of hours. There is one elk that I want to try, and find." Brent told them as he looked around for any signs of his elk.

"No way, in a couple of hours you won't be able to get out of here. It's not safe to stay here any longer." Another one of the guys told him.

"I'll be fine. You guys know that. I've been in way worse of situations than this one, and I've still come out unscathed." Brent argued with them.

All of the guys looked uncomfortable with Brent's decision. Everyone, but Brent moved into a little group, and chatted about the situation. A few minutes later they broke apart looking defeated. They all knew that Brent was going to go anyways.

"Fine, but if you are not back in three hours, we will be sending out a search party for you. I don't care if in three hours you have the elk or not, you are to be back at the hotel. Don't do anything stupid because if you do your dad will come up here and hide my ass for letting you Got it?" Barry said—he was Brent's dads' buddy.

"I do. I'll be back in three hours whether I have the elk or not." Brent confirmed with them.

"Now be careful, not stupid. I know you boy, I know you are capable of doing stupid shit... Just don't." Barry told him.

Brent nodded, and watched as the guys all got in their trucks, and departed.

He had three hours to get his prize, and get out. Which should be a pretty easy task. Now he just had to go back to where he lost the elk, and go from there.

It took him about twenty minutes to find the spot, and then he used his tracking skill the rest of the way. About an hour and a half into his search he heard a rustle, and then saw the head of an elk pop up.

It was his prize.

As quickly as he could he moved towards the elk so he could get a better shot. He used a boulder to hide himself from view. To the left of the boulder there was a twenty foot cliff, and Brent made sure he was as far away from it as he could be.

The elk bent his head down looking for food, and then raised it up again. That was when Brent took his shot. He quickly adjusted his scope, and aimed for its neck. He pulled the trigger and the bullet hit the elk, but it wasn't down for the count yet. He aimed again and this time the elk went down.

Then all hell broke loose a mountain line jumped out behind Brent. He turned around and started to back up towards the cliff. When the lion lunged Brent shot it in the head, and it went down, but it was too late it had already lunged, and knocked him of the edge of the cliff.

Brent and the mountain lion hit the ground. When Brent impacted with the rock the wind was knocked out of him, and he heard the crunch, and snap of a couple of his own bones.

When he could finally breathe in again it pained him so much that he stopped. It was a clear sign that he'd broken multiple of his ribs when he hit the ground.

A few seconds later he felt an intense pain in his right shoulder, and his right arm. He looked at it and tried to move it but nothing was working which told him that his arm was most likely broken. Luckily enough his arm was in the perfect position for him to put it in a sling, but for him to do that he had to move, and he wasn't ready for that just yet.

He looked to the right of him, and saw the mountain lion lying there next to him dead. Blood was pooling out if the gunshot wound, and beginning to soak the ground that Brent was lying on. Quickly he tried to scoot himself away from the animal, and it's blood, but he was rather slow since every time that he tried to move himself it felt like the pain was swallowing him whole.

He'd have to get his pack off his back. It had some water, aspirin and other necessities for when one was stuck in the woods during the winter—much like himself.

With his left arm he began to try and take his pack off. His teeth were gritted in pain the whole time while he tried not to scream. A long while later and after quite a bit of pain he'd somehow managed to take the pack off.

First he took his night out of one of the pockets on his hunting pants, and pulled a spare shirt that he kept in his pack. He started to cut the shirt up so that he could use it to make a make shift sling.

There were some sticks on the ground and he found one that he could use as a splint for the time being.

He cut the stick to size, and placed it against his arm. Once he had the stick in place he grabbed pieces of the shirt and used them to secure the stick to his arm. By the time he'd finished he was exhausted, but he had to try and fight it.

Brent had no clue if he had a concussion, or if he had any internal bleeding, so falling asleep could be detrimental to his lively hood while he was stuck in the woods.

There were some energy bars in his pack along with one of those little bottles of concentrated energy drink flavoring. He grabbed out one of the bars and scarfed it down. Being stranded and almost dying could make a man kind of hungry. He grabbed his water bottle and drank a swig of water, and then he sprayed some of the energy drink stuff in his mouth—he didn't want to mix it with all of his water since might not always want to drink the energy drink.

Brent grabbed his pack again, and began to shuffle through it. He found both his phone, and his walkie talkie, luckily enough neither of them had been beaten up too bad by his fall.

Quickly he turned on his phone and once it had loaded he let out a string of cuss words. The damn thing had no service, and he couldn't get it to connect to the 3G or the 4G which meant that there was no way for him to get help—at least not for his phone anyways. He turned it off to conserve the battery just in case he was able to find himself a way to get service. The walkie talkie also presented problems. It had a range of about five miles, but all the guys were at least thirty miles—if not more—away from him. He could try it, but the chance of one of them getting the connection was practically impossible.

That was when he remembered that the walkie talkie could connect to the police channels. That might be worth a shot. Who knows maybe a cop would be patrolling the area, and would get his message. The chances of that happening were slim to none, but it was the best option he currently had for help.

He pressed the call button and began to speak, "this is Brent Donovan, I'm currently trapped in Middle Fork about five miles in from the beginning of the south hunting trail! I was attacked by a mountain lion, and now I'm trapped on the ledge of a cliff! I'm requesting immediate help! Once again requesting immediate help!" He let go of the call button, and waited, and waited for someone to call him back, but there was nothing but static.

For hours he waited, and that was when it became apparent that no one was coming to help him. He was stranded on the ledge of a cliff with no help, a limited amount of food and water. With only a dead mountain lion to keep him company, while the storm of the decade was quickly approaching him. Safe to say, he was royally screwed.

*****

It had been over six hours since any of the guys had seen Brent, and there had been no word from him. Barry paced around his room impatiently. He'd told that boy to be careful, and not to do anything stupid. Obviously Brent hadn't given a damn. Now he was most likely in some serious deep shit trouble.

He'd have to contact the authorities, and the forest service telling them that they had a missing hunter stuck in one of the worst storms they'd had in a decade.

The next time Barry saw that boy he was going to tan his hide. That was if Brent's father hadn't already tanned his own. His longtime friend was going to be pissed when he found out that it was Barry that had given Brent the okay to go back in and get that elk. He should have told him no, and dragged him kicking and screaming back to the trucks.

Then they wouldn't be in this predicament, and Barry wouldn't be scared out of his mind for Brent's safety. That boy was like a son to him, and if anything happened to him he'd never forgive himself.

Barry turned the TV off in his room, and grabbed his keys and coat. He left and told the boys where he was going.

When he got outside snow was falling fast and thickly down upon him, and the wind was making it hard to see, not to mention that it was also freezing cold outside.

Barry made his way to his truck, and fired it up. He turned the heat all the way up, and pulled out of his spot. He could barely see a hundred feet ahead of him. The sheriff's station was about a fifteen minute drive from the hotel, and in this weather it would turn into at least a thirty minute drive if not forty-five.

During the drive the conditions of the storm became increasingly worse. They had to find Brent and get him out soon or else that boy would freeze to death out in the woods.

At the station there were a few patrol cars parked out front, but beside that there was no one else there. Barry pulled in next to one of the vehicles, and killed the ignition. He pulled the hood of his coat over his baseball cap.

As he stepped out of the cab of the truck he was assaulted with the freezing cold air and the snow that continued to steadily fall. The ground was a covered already with a good four inches of snow already with a couple more feet to come.

He made his way over to the door of the station, and then walked inside. There was slew of activity going on around him. It looked like they pretty busy with the storm at hand.

He walked up to the secretary. "Hello, ma'am I need to speak with the Sheriff. We have a missing hunter out in Middle Fork during this storm."

The lady looked stunned. "A missing hunter you say?"

"Yes ma'am." He shook his head solemnly.

"Let me tell the sheriff. He should be with you in a couple of minutes." The lady smiled at him, and then she stood and made her way to the sheriff's office.

She was probably in her early fifties with dark brown hair that was beginning to gray at the roots, and she had dark green eyes.

Barry sat in a chair while he waited for her to emerge from the office, and give him an okay to see the sheriff.

The door to the sheriff's office opened a few minutes later, and the secretary exited the room. "The sheriff will now see you," she told him.

He tipped his cap at her in appreciation. "Thank you, ma'am."

She smiled at Barry, and went back to her desk.

Barry felt dread fill him over what he was about to tell the sheriff. He entered the office, and closed the door behind him.

Sheriff Hendricks' held out his hand and Barry shook it, and then he sat down. "How are you sheriff?" He questioned the man.

"I'm fine. How have you been Barry? I haven't seen you since last hunting season. You need to come and visit us more often."

Barry shifted in his seat uncomfortably. "I've been fine up until today. One of my guys has gone missing inside Middle Fork, and I need your help to find him and get 'em out alive."

The sheriff looked distressed by the news. "How long ago did you last see him? And who was he?"

Barry scratched his chin. "I'd say I saw him about seven hours ago around noon today, and he was Brent Donovan."

"Brent Donovan? I've never known that boy to get himself in trouble since he started hunting up here. Have you told his father yet?"

"I haven't."

"I don't blame you. I wouldn't want to be on Bill Donovan's bad side either. That man can get pretty scary and protective when it comes to his family."

"Yeah, I was wondering if we could get a search and rescue together. I know that it's not realistic in this weather, but if we don't act soon we might not find him alive." Barry looked down at his hands, ashamed that he'd let Brent go back in.

"It'll take me a couple hours to get one arranged, but we can't leave him out there alone. I'll find out hose willing to go out in this, and then I'll tell you what I've come up with. Let's just hope Brent can take care of himself for a little while longer."

"Let's hope so. He's a smart boy." Barry said, almost trying to reassure himself.

"Go back to your hotel, Bart. I'll call you once I have everything set up. I'll need your help, along with the guys you were hunting with. Especially since you guys were the last one to see him."

Bart yawned and ran his hand over his face. "Alright… I'll be waiting for you to call." He pointed at Sheriff Hendricks' accusingly, and the sheriff just nodded.

*****

Luke walked up to the Donovan's' door reluctantly. He really didn't want to tell them the news. Brent was missing in Middle Fork, and no one had a clue where he was. And then there also was the fact that there was a blizzard, making everything worse.

He pulled up as quietly as he could in his squad car. Once he'd killed then engine he got out and walked onto the front porch, the floor boards creaking a little as he went.

The door knock was starring him in the face, and suddenly the news that he was going to be giving sat like a lump in his throat. He grabbed the door knock, and slammed it against the door a couple of times.

A few seconds later Anna was standing in front of him.

How could this get any worse…?

Now he had to tell the Anna that the man she loved was MIA. Not something he was looking forward to.

"Hello, Ms. Douglas. May I please come in?" He asked her while he rung his hands together.

"Ah... Of course." She held the door open for him. "Is there anything wrong...?"

Luke wasn't quite sure what to say to that. "Um, where's Ms. Donovan? I'd like to speak to the both of you." He looked unsure of himself as he walked into the living room.

Anna looked at him curiously. "Sure... I'll be back in a minute." The conversation was getting more awkward by the minute.

When Anna came back into the room a moment later Cassie was trailing behind her.

"Well, hello Sheriff Andrews, it's a surprise seeing you here this late at night." Cassie told him.

He nodded his head at Cassie. "I'm sorry to have to tell both of you this," Anna's face fell, she knew what was coming, she'd felt it in her gut. "I'm afraid Brent went missing at around noon today in Middle Fork. Now, the sheriff up there..."

Anna collapsed onto the coach. Brent was missing. Her love was missing...

*****

Sorry for the wait on this chapter!!! I've been so busy with work, and family stuff that I've had no extra time. And my birthday is tomorrow!!! I wouldn't expect another chapter until Friday or Saturday!!

The song on the side is Starts With Goodbye by Carrie Underwood. It's such a goo song! Please, give it a listen!!!

Anyways here it is!!! Please vote & comment!!!

Chapter 21

<hr>

Chapter 21

"Are you okay, Anna?" Cassie asked as she kneeled down next to Anna, she was sitting on the couch with a blank look on her face.

All Anna could was shake her head, 'no' while she starred at the floor in disbelief.

Cassie rubbed Anna's shoulders in a poor effort to comfort her. "Come on please talk to me Anna." She got no reply. "He'll be fine I promise you that. Brent's known for getting himself in deep shit, but he always manages to get out of it in one way, or another."

Anna still wouldn't talk, and so Cassie figured that she was still a bit shell shocked from the news.

Deciding that she probably needed a little time to process everything that was happening, Cassie walked over to Luke, and stood by him while they both watched Anna.

"Do you have any other information? I think Anna needs something more... Something that will give her hopes to believe that my idiot of a brother will be okay."

Luke sighed, and looked back at Anna. "Honestly Cass, I only really know what you guys know. All the information I have is that he's missing and that the Sheriff up there has a search and rescue planned. Other than that I'm pretty in the dark until I get another update."

Cassie nodded her head understanding that there was only so much that he could do. "Do you think you could get one of your deputies to give us a ride up there? I don't trust Anna or me to drive up there, and I know she needs to be there."

"Sure... just let me go radio dispatch for an available deputy." Luke turned around and walked out the door to his squad car.

Cassie went back over to Anna. "I know you feel guilty, and you're going to continue feeling this way until we find him, and assure you that he's okay. But Anna you have to talk to us, we can't help you get through this unless you'll talk to us." She sighed. "I know how you feel, and you can trust me if you want to talk about it..."

That was when Anna finally looked up at her; with little tear tracks going down her face. "I don't want to talk about it right now, Cassie," she sounded so defeated.

"Okay, you don't. But you do have to pack were going to be leaving soon for Middle Fork. One of Luke's deputies going to be driving us up there."

Anna just walked away without saying anything else to Cassie. She climbed up the stairs, and made the journey to her room. Once she was inside she closed the door with her back and collapsed against the door. She cried into her hands for a good fifteen minutes.

Finally she felt slightly better—not whole yet, she wouldn't feel whole again until she knew that Brent was okay. Mindlessly she got up and grabbed a bag and began to stuff her clothes into it. Not caring what she placed inside. When the bag was full she zipped it closed and made her way to the bathroom.

She grabbed all of her toiletries, and brought them back to her room. As she walked it was almost like she wasn't herself. It was like someone was pulling the strings for her. She was going through the motions, but not realizing anything that she was doing.

When she'd gotten all of her things situated. She moved away from her bed and to the window in her room. She put her hands on the window sill and looked outside—she seemed to be finding herself looking outside, to the sky for all of her answers lately.

She found her mid drifting away endlessly. Was Brent okay? Was he going to be okay? Was he cold, hungry, or injured?

Most of all as she stood there she realized that she missed him, and she hoped that he too missed her. It had just about killed her when she'd heard the news about his disappearance. She felt like someone was trying to gut her insides while she was still breathing.

Anna guessed that's what love did to you. It made you worry about the one you loved until you knew they were okay. And most of all it made you miss them like you had never missed anyone else before.

There was a knock on Anna's door bringing her back to reality.

"Come in." Anna yelled to whoever was standing outside of her bedroom.

The door creaked as it was opened, and then Cassie was standing inside of her room.

"All of Luke's deputies are busy," Cassie told Anna, "so he's going to be driving us, but first he has to go back to his place, and get himself some clothes and toiletries before he can accompany us."

"Okay," Anna told her, her voice sounding a little croaky from all the crying that she'd done. "How long will he be?"

"Not long. His house is only about a twenty minute drive from here. So I'd expect him to be back in about an hour."

"Alright, I'll be ready to go when he gets back." Cassie started to retreat, but Anna had something that she had to ask. "Do you think he'll be okay" she asked as she stared down at her hands and tried not bawl her eyes out.

"I don't know Anna," Cassie smiled wearily at her. "I hope he will be, but really I'm freaking out just as much as you are. I really honestly don't know how I'm going to be able to call my parents, and tell them about it."

"You'll find a way, Cass. We both will." Anna sighed and lay down on her bed.

*****

"We'll be arriving at Hobson in a couple of minutes," Luke informed Cassie and Anna.

It was late at night and they were all tired, but none of them would rest until they got some answers about Brent's disappearance.

A few short minutes later they pulled up in front of the Sheriff's office. Luke parked his unmarked squad SUV in one of the spots and then they got out. They'd taken the unmarked SUV to try and not bring to much attention. They didn't want everyone to freak out over Brent's disappearance. No, what they needed was for everyone to stay calm, so that it would be easier to find Brent.

There was a secretary sitting at her desk just inside of the building.

"Hello, ma'am I'm looking for the Sheriff," He shrugged some of the snow off of his jacket, and then showed her his badge.

The lady hoped up immediately. "Sheriff Hendricks has been expecting you. I'll go and tell him you're here, Sheriff…"

"Andrews, ma'am. I'm Sheriff Andrews from Walker."

"Alright then, Sheriff Andrews why don't you all take a seat, and help yourself to some coffee, while I speak with the sheriff." She smiled at them and then, walked into what Luke suspected was Sheriff Hendricks' office.

Luke made himself comfortable in one of the armchairs while Cassie and Anna walked over to the coffee machine.

"Being here is making me extremely nervous," Anna told Cassie as she grabbed a foam cup from the stack by the coffee machine.

"I know. I'm feeling the same way." Cassie grabbed a cup as well. "I hope they know something more than we do."

"I hope so, too," she began filling her cup with coffee. "Everyone will probably start searching tomorrow since the snow is starting to fall a little lighter."

After Cassie had filled her cup, and they'd doctors their coffee with some cream and sugar they went back over to Luke and sat down. Before they had had a chance to get comfortable, Sheriff Hendricks, and the secretary emerged.

Luke immediately stood up, and Cassie and Anna followed suit.

"Hello, Sheriff Andrews, and you two are…?" He asked as he tipped his hat towards Cassie and Anna.

Cassie approached him and shook the Sheriff's hand. "I'm Cassie Donovan, Brent's sister, and this is…" she motioned towards Anna, "Anna Douglas, Brent's girlfriend."

Sheriff Hendricks shook Anna's hand. "Let's got my office we can talk privately in there." His eyes looked tired, as he waved them towards his office.

Once inside the three of them sat down in the seats opposite of the Sheriffs.

Anna was the first one to ask questions. "Is he okay? Do you have an area where you expect to find him? I know how these work my brother went missing when in the woods when he was twelve."

"Um… Miss Douglas we currently have no information on his well-being." Sheriff Hendrix rubbed his eyes with the palms of his hands, and then continued on. "As for his location we do have an area of about ten miles. The only problem is that the terrain is not suitable to be maneuvered with such heavy of snow coming down and then blanketing the ground."

"But it's not too bad that we won't be able to do a search and rescue, right?" Luke asked him.

"It's not too bad, but it's going to be a very dangerous search and rescue to boot."

Anna and Cassie were both comforted by what Sheriff Hendricks was telling them.

"When will you begin the search?" The three of them questioned the Sheriff in unison—or at least semi-unison.

"In the morning, but it won't really start to heat up until tomorrow afternoon."

"Why's that?" Luke asked him while he shifted to sit with his elbows on his knees.

"The extreme weather condition search and rescue team won't be able to make it out here until tomorrow afternoon. So until then we'll have to use what we have, but I won't have anyone taking unneeded risks." He shot them a look that could make a person wish that they were buried six feet under.

"I knew your daddy," He continued and looked at Luke, "and he told me about all the stupid shit you did when you were still in school. Hell, even when you were in college."

Luke blushed slightly, "Yes sir, but that man is still one of my own and my friend." He slumped back in his chair. "So I'm not making any promises..."

Sheriff Hendricks shot him a murderous look. "Fine, but if you get your ass in trouble, too, them I'm going to leave your ass where it lays."

"Understood," Luke told him as he shook his head 'yes'.

*****

The next morning it was gloomy outside, and the snow was still coming down steadily, with no news on when it was going to end. None of them has really slept the night before. They'd all tossed and turned while they'd worried about Brent's wellbeing.

When they'd gotten to the hotel after their chat with Sheriff Hendricks they'd gotten rooms. Luke had his own room and Anna and Cassie had gotten a room with two queen beds to share. Although, Anna had opted to sleep in Brent's room where she could smell his scent, and see his things which had given her an odd sense of security. During the night she'd cried into his pulling, and when she awoke she could barely drag herself away from it, but she had to find Brent.

It wasn't a want, it was a need.

After a quick breakfast, and a cup of to go coffee they were all on their way in Luke's squad SUV.

When they arrived at the Middle Fork hunting parking lot it was set up to be a mini portable search and rescue headquarters. Sheriff Hendricks was there barking orders at everyone. They had a couple people with search and rescue husky and malamutes.

Sheriff Hendricks walked over to Luke, Cassie and Anna when he noticed them. He nodded in approval when he saw that they were all wearing the proper attire for a search and rescue during the winter time, and he noticed that they each had packs with things that they would need.

"Are you ready to go searching for Brent?" Sheriff Hendricks asked them, and the three nodded.

Luke pointed at the little headquarters when he saw Barry standing in it. "I'm going to go over there and get some information about what's going on, and see what all Barry know since he is the one who reported Brent missing," He told them, and then walked away leaving Cassie and Anna standing there with the Sheriff.

"When will we start looking for Brent?" Anna asked him.

"As soon as we get everyone breached about what's going on," He scrubbed a hand over his face, and then looked at Anna. "Can I talk to you privately for a moment?"

Anna nodded at the Sheriff, and then they walked away from Cassie. "What did you want to talk to me about?"

"I wanted to make sure that you're okay to do this search. I mean I have a daughter, and when things went down with her fiancé she had a hard time functioning, and I just wanted to make sure that you're going to be okay. I need to know that your emotions won't influence you to make a bad decision." When he saw the look of annoyance on her face he decided that he had to change his approach. "What I'm trying to say is that I care, and I'm not willing to let anyone else risk their wellbeing."

Anna tried to smile, but it turned it more of a grimace. "I can assure you that my emotions will not affect my ability to look for Brent. I've done this before once when my brother went missing in the woods connected to my house, and my emotions did not affect me in that situation, either."

The Sheriff held his hands up in surrender. "I just wanted to make sure. Now go over and get Cassie and then head over to the headquarters we have set up over there. I need to get everyone breached so that we can start this thing."

Anna couldn't deny it she liked Sheriff Hendricks. He reminded her of her father before things went bad between them. But thinking of her family now would only complicate things, and she had far more important things to be thinking about. Like Brent.

Cassie waited patiently as Anna trudged back to her. "What'd he want to talk to you about, Anna?" She asked when Anna was right by her.

"Nothing really... He just wanted to talk to me about my search and rescue skills." Anna told her, but Cassie could tell that Anna was not telling her everything. Cassie couldn't figure out why she was starting to put up walls to guard herself.

"Okayyy..." Cassie wanted to pry, but this was neither the time nor the place to do it.

Anna rubbed her arms when some wind blew by her and left a chill in her bones. "Let's just go over there," she pointed towards the search and rescue headquarters, "and get done with the meeting and them we can go and search for Brent."

"Sure, let's go and get this thing started."

The two of them approached the headquarters, and found places to sit. Unfortunately the benches were metal, and when they sat down it was quite chilly.

"Okay, now that we have everyone here let's get started." Sheriff Hendricks' began to breach everyone along with Luke's help. "We have a Caucasian male that went missing last night. He's in his late twenties. He's approximately six foot three, weighing probably a couple pounds under two hundred. He has brown hair and gray eyes with a muscled build."

It was now Luke's turn to break in. "The last time he was seen was around noon yesterday where we currently are. He was supposed to be back by noon, but he never returned. We have a ten mile search radius that we are looking at. For the time being we are only allowing you all to search two miles in. Later when the other search and rescue people come we will start to cover more ground. We want you all to be prepared because this may very well end up being a search and retrieve. We hope it doesn't come to that, but right now with the information we have anything is possible."

"We have walkie talkies at the table to the far left," Sheriff Hendricks pointed ad he spoke, "along with trackers that you will all be wearing so that we know where you are at all times. We have maps that will be handed out once I'm finished talking. That will also be when you find out who your partner will be. The groups will consist of two people and one of the dogs. Let's get started. May God be with you all." The Sheriff finished up, and walked off.

Another search and rescue person came up and began speaking. "Listen up. I have the group assignments. Sheriff Andrews will be partnered with Anna Douglas, their K-9 will be Kenai…" That's all Anna heard. She would've thought that she'd be partnered up with Cassie.

Anna got up from her seat with Cassie and Luke trailing after her. She was on a mission to talk to Sheriff Hendricks.

He was sitting at one of the command tables with a computer when Anna found him. "Excuse me, but I thought my partner was going to be Cassie." Anna told him as she gave him a glare. By then Cassie and Luke were standing by her.

"You were until I was made privy to the knowledge that she's pregnant." Cassie and Anna both gasped.

"Who told you?" Cassie asked him none too kindly. He pointed over at Luke.

"Luke told me while you and Anna were on your way over here. I will not have you looking for your brother if it means bringing a risk to an un born child, and my dear this is a high risk search and rescue. Don't worry though you'll be here with me tracking everyone, and the information we are made privy to."

Cassie was none too happy about this development. She stalked over to Luke. "Who told you?"

Luke blushed, and if Cassie hadn't been so made she would have thought it cute. He cleared his throat. "Uhhh… Jess told me the other day when I was at her store." He scratched his head, completely uncomfortable with the turn the conversation had made.

Once Cassie had walked off Anna broached a conversation with Luke. "Loos like you're going to be my partner."

*****

Sorry about the wait for this chapter... I've been supper busy and when I was writing it seemed like nothing was coming out right. It's a little over three thousand words, and I know it's kind of a filler, but it was necessary. I hope it was worth the wait. There will be some Brent in the next chapter.

The song on the side is Mine Would Be You by Blake Shelton. I thought it was a good song about Brent and Anna's relationship. Please give it a listen!

Thanks for reading! Please vote and comment!!!

Chapter 22

C hapter 22

Brent was freezing his ass off—quite literally too, he'd looked, it was now a mighty fine shade of blue. And there was also the fact that his arm felt like it was going to kill him from the amount of pain that it elicited. And he had to admit lying next to that dead mountain lion was a bit creepy. Safe to say he kept his distance from the damn thing.

Having only a dead mountain lion for companionship made him miss Anna even more than he already did, and the comfort that always came with her. Lying next to her the night before he left for his hunting trip was the closest he'd come to Heaven, not to mention the best night of sleep he'd ever had.

It'd been about a day since his little incident, it sounded better that way. He couldn't help but glare over at the damn mountain lion. If hadn't been for that stupid thing he'd have his elk, and he'd be heading home on time. Not to mention that he wouldn't have multiple broken or fractured bones, and probably a couple more dislocated.

As much as he wanted lay the brunt of the blame on the mountain lion he knew that he had to leave quite a bit of it for himself. He knew that he was the main person to blame for his stupidity. He never should have gone back for the elk.

By now that had to be searching for him, or at least he hoped that they were. He wasn't quite sure if they'd be able to get to him though. It had snowed at least two more feet since his incident, and he was sure that maneuvering through Middle Fork with all the snow was just about impossible with your basic search and rescue team. Maybe they'd called in one of the severe weather teams.

God, he hoped they had. He didn't know if he would be able to survive out her with only a little water, a couple protein bars, and one of those survival blankets for too long. He'd been lucky enough to have fallen onto a ledge that had a small area that was hallow enough for him to take cover under.

"Holy shit! Damn! F*ck!" Brent groaned when he shifted to grab his pack. The cold weather did nothing but intensify the ache and pain he felt radiating from his body.

He gritted his teeth as he dug around in search of his small bag filled with personal items.

Call him a sap, or whatever. But Brent always carried pictures of his family with him. You never knew when you'd get homesick, and miss the people you loved the most. Especially the girl that carried your heart with her all day long, and she probably didn't even know it...

That was unless she'd heard him when he'd told her while she was asleep...

Well, shit...! That wasn't how he had wanted to tell her. What if she had heard him!

He'd just have to hope that she hadn't heard him. He had to tell her when the time was right. And right now it was not. He wanted to tell her when this whole thing was done, when he was recovered or at least mostly recovered.

He looked at the picture she had sent him at the beginning of this crazy journey. She was just breath taking he knew that he'd never get tired of looking at her face. His eyes roamed down the picture and then they fell on his lips. Oh, how he'd love to be able to kiss them right now...

That was the moment when he knew that he'd be okay. He'd be okay because hopefully he'd have Anna waiting for him. He knew that their life wouldn't always be pretty, but he'd work through their future and current rough patches because he knew that if he always had her love then he would be a man with a lot to be thankful and happy for.

He looked up at the sky and saw more snow starting to fall down it was going to be a long while till they found him yet. Brent closed his eyes and let sleep take him. He had to have just a few minutes of sleep... just a few he told himself....

*****

"I'm going to tell you right now. I will be taking whatever risks that are needed to get Brent back safe and sound, or at least mostly safe." Anna gave Luke a take no shit look that almost had him shaking in his boots.

He just nodded his head at her. "Don't worrying, I will be taking the risks needed to," he paused. "Well that is unless you almost get yourself killed. Then the terms will change."

Anna stayed silent while she led their search and rescue K-9, Kenai through the brush that was covered in thick, heavy snow. The dog just clomped along happily as if he had never had more fun in his life. It seemed like the search was a game for him, one that he wanted to conquer and then be rewarded for when he found the missing human.

"He's quite the dog isn't he?" Luke asked her as they covered more ground.

"He is. Aren't you Kenai?" She asked the dog and he stopped sniffing the ground, and looked up long enough to wag his tail at her. Anna grabbed a treat out of the pouch on her waist and fed it to him before they continued on.

"Do you think he'll be okay, Luke? I keep hoping that he will, but what if something happened to him"—she chocked on a sob and had to keep a tight hold on her emotions, as to not start crying—"I mean he was out her with a gun what something happened and it miss fired..."

Her eyes were misted with tears, and Luke could see that they were teetering close to spilling over. He grabbed Kenai's leash from her, and then turned to face her. "Don't think like that. You're just going to get yourself all worked up, and then you won't be of any help to Brent." He warned her.

Anna took a couple deep breaths, feeling a little more in control of herself now. "Okay..." she breathed out and then continued, "how much ground have we covered?"

"Only about a mile and a half, I don't suspect to find him until were about three or four miles in."

Anna sighed. It felt like they were so close to him, but yet so far away.

"I just want to find him," she whined. "I can't stand being away from him."

Luke looked over at her and studied her face. She was most definitely in love with Brent. He could see it in her eyes. He honestly felt bad for her, not because she loved Brent, but because they couldn't find him. That must have be hell on the heart for her. He honestly didn't know what he would do if he loved someone and couldn't find them. He'd probably go bat shit crazy.

Static and then a voice came through the walkie talkie bringing Luke back from his wandering thoughts. "Team Kenai, we need you to come back to search and rescue headquarter. The other team has arrived, and is ready to begin."

Luke held the device up to his mouth and then pressed the call button. "This is team Kenai. We hear you loud and clear. We will begin to make our way back. Expect us in a about a half an hour or so."

"Looks like we're heading back, we should probably be able to begin searching again in about an hour or two." Luke informed Anna.

She huffed and puffed a little not wanting to leave the path they were searching cold, but then she kicked it into high gear and they made it back in a sufficient amount of time.

*****

Brent heard a rustling noise, and the sound of people's voices, bringing him out of his slumber. He was barely able to look around his eye sight was foggy, and his mind was all jumbled up making him not be able to think coherently.

He heard the sweet melodic voice of someone so dear to him. Could it be? Was his mind just playing a trick on him?

It was Anna. The woman he loved more than life itself. This wasn't fake and his brain was certainly not at all trying to play a trick on him. It felt so good know in that she was there to help him. That he was going to make it out alive with her help.

Brent blinked a few times rapidly and his eye sight got a little bit better.

"Brent. Brent are you okay!" He heard Anna yelling. Although he loved the sound of her voice it was making his head pound.

"Anna," he croaked out the sound barely audible that he was surprised that she had heard it.

He could faintly see her turning to the two other people that she was with. He didn't know who they were, and he really honestly didn't care just as long as she didn't go away.

"Someone is going to repel down to you Brent," she told him in her sweet voice. "The rescue helicopter is on its way. You're going to be okay." He heard her choke out as if she was beginning to cry from relief.

"Anna... Stay with me..." His mind began to fade on him and then everything was black. His body had finally given up from sheer mental and physical exhaustion.

*****

It took them longer back at the search and rescue headquarters than Anna would have liked, but now they had another person to assist them in looking for Brent.

"It looks like I will be on your team for the remainder of the search." A man in his mid-thirties with a muscular build told them as he approached.

"Sounds good," Luke told the guy. "My name's Luke Andrews and this is Anna Douglas," Luke told him pointing at Anna.

The man held out his hands to both of them, while he kept his dark green eyes on them. "Nice to meet both of you, I'm Derek Wellington." They shook hands, and pulled on their packs.

"Let's get going." Anna advised them and then she let Derek take the lead along with Kenai.

The hike was even more daunting now. It was starting to get colder, and there was some more snow falling, but not enough to make the search too dangerous to continue on with.

Luke started a conversation with Derek after they'd been hiking for about an hour, and a half. "How long have you been doing this kind of search and rescue?" Luke asked him as they trudged on.

"A little over ten years, I like it though it adds a little extra something to my day to day life. I actually know Brent, we went to high school together, but I moved away shortly after graduation."

Anna and Luke's eyes both shot to Derek in surprise.

"You knew him?" Anna gasped. Derek just nodded his head his dark brown hair slightly falling into his eyes.

"Wait..." Luke looked at Derek deep in thought. "I remember you, everyone used to call you..."

"Derek the Brace Face." Derek finished Luke's sentence for him.

"Yeah, man I'm sorry about that," Luke apologized. High school had been awful for all of them. "But you've obviously gotten past those awkward teenage years."

"Thanks, but I'm over it. I have straight teeth and I'm no longer chubby so I'm fine." Derek told them.

Anna had trouble imagining Derek as chubby. He looked like he'd been in shape his whole life.

A few minutes later Kenai, who'd been happy to just follow the scent he'd been given to look for, went crazy. He was barking and running around in circles towards a destination. Derek was having hell of a time trying to control the dog.

"Look around you guys," Derek yelled to them, "I think Kenai's found something."

Anna's heart was beating a mile a minute.

They were close. They were so close to finding Brent!

Anna looked around, and then took off. There was a ledge about four hundred feet away from her, and for some reason she felt like she needed to be over there, so she hauled her ass.

Anna fell to her knees at the edge of the ledge, breathing hard, and sweating like no other under her winter gear.

When she looked down her breath fled from her body, and her heart stopped beating for a moment.

Brent...

She'd found Brent...

"I found him..." Anna turned and yelled toward Luke and Derek.

"What?!" They both yelled, and then the realization hit them, they'd found Brent. And then they both started to haul as towards Anna.

"Brent!" Anna yelled down to him, not sure if he could hear her. "Brent, are you okay?!"

Anna wasn't quite sure if her mind was playing a trick on her, but she could have sworn that he he'd said, "Anna." It sounded like he was tired, and the sound was barely audible.

She looked down and she could see him laying down with his eyes open. His face was scrunched up as if he was in pain.

"He said my name... I heard him..." She turned toward Luke and Derek, and informed them, since they were now next to her.

Derek immediately took control of the situation, and began giving out orders. This is what he'd been trained to do. "Anna I need you to talk to him, and keep him calm while I call for the rescue helicopter, and Luke gets out the repelling equipment."

Anna nodded 'okay' at him. She didn't know how alert Brent was.

"Someone is going to repel down to you Brent." She told him, all of the sudden getting a giant lump in her throat and having to try not to cry. "The rescue helicopter is on its way. You're going to be okay."

It all became too much for Anna and she began to cry from the stress she'd felt for that last week, and because she was so relieved and happy that they'd found him.

She could hear the guys behind her getting all the stuff ready a radio a bunch of different people, but she also looked down at Brent and heard him say something to her. "Anna... stay with me..."

It sounded like he was too weak to speak, and then she looked down at him again. To find that he was laying there with his eyes closed, and his stomach was barely rising from his breathing.

"Brent!!!" she screamed over, and over again. It wasn't fair! She'd just found him, and now he wasn't responding... Tears flowed in trails down her cheeks from her despair.

Derek and Luke realized what had happened at were at her side almost immediately. Luke bent down and hauled her into his arms, and let her cry on his shoulder.

Luke used his walkie talkie to radio in a message. "Brent is not responding. I repeat he is not responding. We need that helicopter now. Derek is going to repel down to him now. I repeat we need the helicopter, a man's life depends on it."

Derek looked at the repelling gear and then at Luke. "Let me get the harness on and then I'll go down to him. Luke I'm going to need you up here holding the rope, and guiding me down. You're going to have to let go of Anna."

Luke nodded and let go of Anna, but he handed her his walkie talkie. "Use this to call Cassie, and let her know what's going on. I have to help Derek, maybe she can help comfort you."

Anna took the walkie talkie from him and nodded.

Luke approached Derek and put on the other harness, and then helped him get all the set up. As Derek got ready to repel down to Brent Luke began to whisper to him. "I need you to go down there to help him because if he is not okay. Anna is going to be a wreck. Whatever you find out about Brent's condition I want you to radio it in because I don't want Anna knowing if he dies, or at least right now. She can't handle any more stress at the moment. She's at her breaking point already as it is."

Derek nodded, and then eased himself over the edge of the ledge, beginning to repel his way down to Brent.

*****

I'm sorry about the wait for this chapter. I just started school again, and I have been working out like crazy. I've been at a plateau so I've been having to overcome that. :(

Sorry about the ending... Another cliffhanger... Sorry, I hope you enjoyed the chapter. The song on the side is Bless The Broken Road by the Rascal Flatts. It's a great song.

Please vote and comment!!! Thanks for reading!!!

Chapter 23

Chapter 23

Derek's boot hit the floor of the ledge with a clump. He wasn't quite sure what he would find, but he sure wasn't expecting to see a dead mountain lion lying near, Brent who was clearly unresponsive.

Derek unhooked his harness from the rope, and stepped over to Brent. He bent down and tried to shake him, seeing if he could get him to respond. Then he checked for breathing, but he couldn't find anything.

Damn it! This wasn't what he'd expected to find! He'd been told it would be a search and rescue, not a possible search and retrieve...

He had to pull himself together. He was no help to Brent if he stayed in his thoughts. He had minutes to save his life, and right now it was turning into seconds.

There was no pulse! He didn't have time to check for other injuries. He had to start compressions and breaths. It was just too bad he didn't have an AED. That would have helped him a ton.

Derek stripped Brent's chest, and still got no response. Brent really was gone...

No he couldn't think about that. He stripped off his gloves as the adrenaline began to pump through his veins.

He placed his hands on Brent's chest and began compressions. "One... two... three...!" he counted out loud. He made his hands begin working to a rhythm. Once he finished his first set of thirty compressions he quickly grabbed the barrier he always kept with him and placed it on Brent's mouth.

He gave him two quick breaths that made Brent's chest rise. He then started on compressions again counting in his head, they were surprisingly easy, but he guessed that Brent had had a few broken ribs before he'd started compressions.

He radioed the new information on Brent's condition to headquarters. "I have an update on Brent Donovan! He is non-responsive and I am currently doing CPR! We need that helicopter even sooner now!"

He finished that set of compressions, and then continued on with the rest until he'd finished five sets. He checked his carotid for a pulse, but he didn't find anything.

Damn! He started another set of compressions even though his hands were beginning to ache from his exertion, but he soldiered on.

Once he finished another set of compressions he immediately did two more rescue breaths. He finished the set of the five sets, and then he stopped.

He didn't know what he'd do if he found no pulse, again.

He took one deep breath, and then placed his fingers on Brent's neck, and he found a pulse. It was barely there, but it was a pulse.

Thank, God! He checked for breathing and there was barely anything there, but it was there.

He grabbed a fresh survival blanket from his pack, and covered Brent with it, while he watched his vital signs closely.

"Brent is breathing on his own now, and his pulse is there, but it's not great! I really need that helicopter! He's not out of the woods yet!" Derek reported into his walkie talkie.

What was taking so long? The helicopter should have been here by now. It'd been fifteen minutes since they'd made the requested for it.

He might as well check for other injuries while he waited.

*****

Anna sat there silently while Derek was on the ledge helping Brent. She was starting to get annoyed. Luke wouldn't let her sit near the ledge, or do anything to help for that matter.

He claimed that he didn't need her to be near anything close to Brent at the moment.

Who the hell did he think he was to be making decisions for her? She was her own person, and she could sure as hell decide where she wanted to be. And right now she wanted to be with Brent more than anything else in this world.

Anna got up from where she sat and went over to the ledge while Luke wasn't paying attention. She watched Derek compressing his hands against Brent's chest.

What the...

What was going on?!

Then she saw Derek bend over and give Brent two breaths.

Brent wasn't responding? She'd thought that he'd just fallen asleep from exhaustion. Not from his heart and breathing stopping.

Anna wanted to start panicking at that moment, but she had no more panic left in her. She was utterly emotionally and physically exhausted.

"Luke," she croaked, "what's going on down there?"

Luke took one look at her, and then over the ledge. "Uh, nothing, don't worry about it Derek knows what he's doing." Luke's face betrayed him he didn't look okay. He knew that there was something seriously wrong going on. Derek shouldn't have had to do CPR on Brent. This was not the way the search was supposed to be going.

He knew that something was wrong, but he wasn't going to let Anna know that.

"Everything will be fine. Let's just wait for the helicopter to get here." Luke's voice sounded anything but sure about what he was saying while he tried to comfort her for a couple of minutes.

Luke moved away from Anna and grabbed his walkie talkie with a shaking hand. He radioed Derek hoping that the situation down there really wasn't as bad as it looked.

"Hey, man what's going on down there?" Luke questioned Derek.

I took a few minutes, but he got a response. "When I got down here Brent was unresponsive—no breathing or pulse—so I started to do CPR. His pulse is back now, it's slow, but it's starting to become steady, and he's breathing fairly well on his own."

"So he's okay now?" Luke asked Derek.

"I wouldn't say he's okay, but he's most definitely alive. It seems that he had a couple of broken ribs before I started compressions, but he has a couple more now. I just assed the rest of his injuries and it seems that he either has a broken shoulder it's dislocated. He has some pretty deep scratches on his arms, and body from where the mountain lion attacked him.

"We're going to have to wait until we get him to the hospital find out what else is wrong, but I was able to find those pretty easily."

Brent's injuries didn't sound too good, but the man was alive so everything wasn't lost yet. "How long until the helicopter gets here?" Luke questioned Derek.

"I'd say another five minutes, and then they'll be here." Derek hoped that was the case, because even though Brent had a pulse and was breathing the man was not out of the woods out yet. He didn't if Brent would make it too much longer without the medical care the flight for life team would provide.

"Should I tell Anna about Brent, and everything that's wrong with him?" Luke asked Derek needing some else's oinion because he had no clue what to do.

"Probably, I would be pissed if someone wouldn't tell me what was going on with the person I love."

"Fair enough. I'll see you when the helicopter gets here." Luke put his walkie talkie in his pocket.

"Anna I think we need to talk." Luke told her while she just looked over at him with a scared expression on her face.

*****

Anna felt relief flood her body. It wasn't as bad as it had looked. Brent was going to make it. She felt like crying, but she' didn't think she had anymore tears to shed.

"Can I go with him when they get here?" Anna asked Luke.

"I'm not sure we'll have to ask them when they get here," Luke didn't think they would, but there was no reason to crush her heart again after it had finally had a chance to rebound.

Just then they heard the hum of a helicopter approaching. Anna almost started jumping around like a child that just received its first horse. "Do you hear that?! The helicopter is coming! Brent's going to be okay!" Anna jumped up and hugged Luke.

He hugged Anna back, and then put her back on her feet. "Down tiger, he's not out of the woods yet. Let's just signal them in."

Anna nodded her head in agreement, and then she pulled out a flare and shot it away from the helicopter, signaling her position while she yelled and waved her arms around like a mad woman.

Luke did the same and together they helped the helicopter safely land. The door on the side opened and two people dressed in flight suits stepped off of the twin engine helicopter with supplies in their hands.

The two people ran over to Anna and Luke. "Where's the patient." The first one yelled over the roar of the helicopter.

Anna and Luke pointed over to the ledge, and the rescue crew frowned, but walked over anyways.

They looked down at Brent and immediately began working on unloading their equipment. One ran back to the helicopter and crabbed a back board that could be hooked up to a rope to pull Brent up from the ledge.

Quickly they worked together to assemble the repelling gear, and then one of them had begun repelling while the other got ready to lower down the equipment.

Anna couldn't believe it. They'd barely been there for ten minutes and they were already getting ready to rescue Brent, and then take him to the hospital.

A couple minutes later the man standing with Anna and Luke pulled out his walkie talkie and listened for a couple seconds and then he began to lower down the back board and the bag that Anna could only assume was filled with medical supplies.

Anna couldn't help herself she sat by the ledge and watched what they were doing. Derek was down there helping the guy put Brent on the back boards. They put a neck brace around Brent neck, and fastened him onto the board. The whole thing was intriguing to Anna, but she couldn't help but focus on Brent. He didn't look good. He looked so pale and battered that Anna had to wonder if he could get better because from her view he looked dead. She knew he wasn't, but that still didn't change the way he looked.

"I'm going to need your help." The guy looked at Luke, and motioned for him to come over, and Luke complied. "I need you to help pull me up them up."

Luke grabbed the rope and began to tug, and pull as well as he could. His muscles screamed at him a little. Now Luke could bench a good two hundred pounds, but still. Brent needed to lay off the doughnuts or whatever he liked to eat.

They continued to pull until they'd pulled Brent and the rescuer and Brent to the top of the ledge. Anna went over and helped to pull Brent onto the ground near the ledge, and then she continued to unhook him from the rope so that they could pull the other guy up the rest of the way.

Once they were up Luke moved away and helped to pull Derek up.

The two rescuers picked up all the equipment and put it back in the helicopter, and then they loaded Brent in.

Anna ran over to them. "Can I come with you?"

They shook their heads. "I'm sorry miss, but I can't let you come with us it's against protocol."

"I don't give a shit if it's protocol that man is all I have, and I need to be with him."

"Once again I'm sorry miss, but we can't. There are others back at the headquarters that can take you with them to the hospital."

Anna was fuming, but there was nothing she could do. they wouldn't budge. "Fine, just take care of him. Can I give him a kiss real quick."

The two men looked back and forth at each other, and then the one she'd been talking to spoke up. "Alright, but make it quick."

Anna nodded at them and then leaned over to Brent, and caressed his cheek. "I love you," she whispered and one lone tear fell onto his face, and Ann whipped them away. "Don't leave me, I need you too much." She kissed his cheek lightly, and then she gave him a sweet kiss on his lips. "Bye, I'll see you soon." She took one more look and then sniffled as she began to walk away from the helicopter so that they could take off.

Anna walked straight over to Derek and Luke. They both pulled her in and gave her a bear hug.

"He'll be okay. Don't worry." Derek told her, as her tears continued to fall.

*****

A few long hours later Anna was at Benefits Hospital in Great Falls. When she had arrived they'd led her to a waiting room for people that were waiting for a loved one in surgery. Cassie was by her side while they waited. Brent's parents were also due to arrive any minute, and Anna was waiting nervously for them.

Anna and Cassie were huddled up on the couch trying not to worry too much.

A few minutes earlier Luke and Sheriff Hendricks had left after debriefing them and getting Anna's statement.

No one would tell her anything other than Brent had been rushed into emergency surgery for a punctured lung after he'd arrived. He'd received the puncture from a bone while Derek was doing CPR to save his life. Anna didn't blame him though, he'd saved Brent and if it wasn't for him they'd be mourning Brent's death instead of waiting for him to get out of surgery. They also had to do something about his fractured shoulder.

He'd been in the operating room for a good two hours and they'd said it'd take another two hours or so to repair his shoulder. Anna just couldn't wait for him to get out so that she could tell him that she loved him again.

She'd never been so sure of anything before. All the doubts Leslie had placed in her mind were gone. She wanted Brent forever. He was her one true love, and she was going to take advantage of that. She wanted everything with him the white picket fence, the kids, and most of all the love they shared.

She'd be able to tell him soon. Soon she'd have everything she'd ever dreamed of.

*****

So how'd you like it?

I've decided to give Chrissie her owns story and it's going to come before Cassie's. Please don't hate me... *I say as I cringe in fear* I'm not exactly sure what it's going to be called. I'm thinking it'll be called: The Unexpected Bride, but I'm not sure. It will center around Chrissie and Derek.

I know my imagination is too active for my own good. Derek captured my heart, and I couldn't just let him go, and then I thought about how Chrissie didn't have a beau and the two together, and now we have another story. Oh yeah, Derek will be played by... DUH DUH DUH... Jared Padalecki, but that might change to Paul Walker. I haven't decided. Tell me which of the two you think it should be.

On another note. OMG!!! Anna said she loved him!!! *grins like a little girl* I just love those two so much! Anyways the song on the side is What A Beautiful Day by Chris Cagle. I love that song!

Please vote and comment!!! Thank you guys for reading!!!!!!! I love you all!!!!!!!!!!!!!!

Chapter 24

C hapter 24

A little while later Anna and Cassie still sat in the waiting room, except now there were more people waiting with them.

Cassie and Brent's parents had arrived and were both emotional wrecks—like everyone else—waiting for news on their son's condition.

When they'd arrived Anna had ran up to them and just started crying.

"We fought," she whimpered, "and then he went on that trip and I just feel so awful. I'm so sorry." She sobbed out, her throat quickly betraying her by closing so that she couldn't talk anymore.

Brent's mother wrapped her arms around Anna and they cried together while Cassie was tucked in her father's arms doing the same. It took a few minutes for them to stop crying and when everyone stepped away. Anna noticed that Bill had unshed tears in his eyes.

That was a father's love if she'd ever seen it. Only a man who loved his son would be able to stand there with tears in his eyes and not be embarrassed.

Bill went over to Anna and gave her a bear hug. "It's not your fault. My boy has the hardest head around. Nothing will get through his thick skull."

Anna laughed a little, but it hurt her heart so she stopped. "I just feel so bad, we fought and then he left. We didn't even have a chance to make up." Anna's lips were trembling as she spoke and tried so hard not to cry. "And then I saw him on the ledge and..."

Denise and Bill looked at her with a shocked expression on their faces. "You fought? What happened?" Denise asked, it was obvious that she was confused.

Why would they fight they were so perfect together, and for each other.

"Leslie showed up, and she kissed him. I lost it. I thought he was going back to Leslie." Anna should have known when that Brent would never cheat on her especially not with Leslie after all she'd put him through.

Bill frowned and Denise looked pissed. "I told him that that girl was no good for him, but he wouldn't listen to me. I should have known she'd try to come back. I should have warned you, but I didn't think about it."

"It's okay Denise. Leslie confessed to everything and even apologized." Denise looked shocked. "I know I was surprised too. I was going to talk to Brent about everything before he left, but I didn't get the chance."

Denise frowned. "Well, you can't help everyone. I'm glad that she at least apologized, but I still don't like that girl."

Anna smiled at her. "I don't either. After Leslie did what she did, Brent tried to make me hear him out, but I wouldn't. I was so hurt, and I just couldn't do it. I didn't even get a chance to tell him I was sorry before he left. I love him so much..." Anna's eyes began to well up again.

This time it was Bill who comforted Anna. "He'll be okay, and from what they said when we came in, he's doing alright. He may be as cranky as a bear for a while, but he'll be fine." Bill gave her a bear hug. "My son's a fighter, and I'm sure that he loves you. He won't give up when he has the woman he loves waiting for him."

Did he really love her?

Anna dearly hoped so because if he didn't Anna didn't know what she'd do.

Anna embraced Bill back and then stepped away. "Thanks, that was exactly what I needed to hear."

*****

"Hello, is this Brent Donovan's family?" Asked a tired looking doctor in surgery scrubs asked them.

Denise's head popped from where it had been laying on Bill's chest. "Yes, I'm his mother."

"I'm Doctor Simmons, and I was the one to perform the surgeries on our son." He shook hands with each of them. "I'm pleased to tell you that Brent is a very lucky man, and that the surgery went well. He should be fine. You'll be able to see him once he's out of recovery," he looked down at the watch on his wrist, "in about another hour when we have him moved out of recovery."

The four of them stood up, and all three of the woman hugged the doctor. Bill gave him a handshake.

"Where will he be?" Anna asked the doctor.

"He will have a room in the ICU, and if he does well tonight and stays stable then most likely late tomorrow afternoon they'll move him into a regular hospital room. It could be sooner it just depends on how well he's doing."

"Thank you." The four of them said at just about the same time.

The doctor just shook his head. "It was my pleasure. I'll be back here tomorrow to check on Brent and answer any more questions that you might have." The doctor bid them a farewell and then left.

After he had gone they all merged into one giant hug. They were all so relieved that there had been no complication, and that he was doing fine, and on the path to recovery.

Anna continued to sit there with Brent's family until someone came out to tell them that it was okay for them to visit with Brent for a short while.

A young nurse with light blonde hair and green eyes came over to them. "If you would like to come see Mr. Donovan, I can take one of you at a time." She smiled at them.

They all looked at each other and then Bill and Denise shared a look. Then they turned to Anna. "I think that you should go Anna. You need to see him more than the rest of us. You have thinks you need to tell him even if he is unconscious."

Anna looked quite taken back. "I-I couldn't..." she sputtered out.

Cassie smiled at her. "You know she's right, she's always right."

"But I already saw him today before they flew here with him." Anna still had a shocked look on her face.

Bill smiled and chuckled at Anna while the nurse looked at them waiting for an answer on who would go first. "Go," Bill prodded her, "I think that my son would want to see you first anyways."

Anna stood up on legs that were none too steady.

"I'll take you to see him." The petite nurse told her but Anna wasn't paying any attention to her.

"I just want to warn you that there are a lot of tubes and machines hooked up to Mr. Donovan, and it might be alarming."

"Trust me I think I'll be fine." Anna smiled at her. "I've seen him lying on a ledge lifeless." Anna tried to joke it off, but those images were still so fresh, and she needed to see him to know that that wasn't how he was now.

"I guess you're right." The nurse said, as she led Anna into the ICU room.

The room was so pale and dark that it depressed Anna little bit. There was a lone chair sitting next to Brent's bed, and when the nurse said that he was hooked up to countless tubes and machines she really wasn't joking.

He was still so pale, and there were so many things hooked up to him, it seemed like there were too many.

"I'll go ahead and leave you here with him. If you notice any changes or have any questions just holler and someone will come, I'll be back in ten minutes." The nurse started to walk away, but then it seems as if she remembered something. "Just a warning he might wake up and talking to them helps, but just a fair warning he might remember whatever you say when he wakes up," and just like that the nurse was gone.

Anna went over and sat in the chair. She wasn't quite sure what to do so she grabbed his hand careful not to bump the IV in it. She kissed his hand

and one lone tear fell from her eyes and onto his hand, but she kissed it away.

"You had me so worried," she tried to laugh it off make it seem like it wasn't a big deal. "I don't know what I would have done if I had lost you. I almost did you know, you died on me for a little while there on the ledge. I was so worried, I saw Derek doing compressions on your chest and I just lost it.

"I'm sorry for everything, you know. I should have believed you, I knew you would never cheat on me nor would you go back to Leslie." She sighed. "I got scared, you're the first man I've truly ever loved, and I couldn't stand it if you hurt me the way my family had. So I pushed you away. I know I shouldn't have, and I know it was wrong of me, but I couldn't help it."

Tears started to flow trails down her cheeks, and she tried her best to wipe them away without having to let go of Brent's hand. "I love you so much, Brent. I love you to the moon and back, infinity." She stood up and kissed him lightly on the cheek, and then she gave him a nice solid peck on the lips since he wasn't on a breathing tube.

She heard him moan, and she laughed through her tears. He didn't wake up, but she knew that he sensed her. "Oh, you like that, huh?" She chuckled. "Well, wake up and there will be many more where that one came from, and also some that will be way better than those."

Anna stayed silent for a few minutes, and just watched Brent's chest rise and fall with the breaths he took while, she listened to the steady beat of his heart on the monitor.

He was going to be okay.

Everything was going to be okay.

"It's time for you to go, Miss." The nurse she'd met earlier told her as she walked into the room.

Anna smiled at her. "Can I say goodbye to him?" she asked.

"Of course, just come out when you're finished." The nurse smiled at her and walked out into the hallway.

Anna kissed Brent's cheek one more time. "I have to go, but I'll be back later." She moved her lips to his ear and whispered, "I love you," before walking away.

*****

Everything was cloudy, it was like a dark mist, and Brent was trying to fight his way back into the world of the living. He wanted to hear his angel's voice again. She'd come to him multiple times before, speaking sweet words of love to him, and even giving him sweet kisses.

She was special, and the reason why he was fighting so hard to become conscious. He wanted to hear more of her voice, see her face he had no doubt that she was the most beautiful thing to have ever walked on this planet. Of that he was sure of, even though he'd never met her.

Or had he? Her voice was awfully familiar, but in his foggy state he couldn't think of who it was so he kept pushing through the dark fog, until he quite literally saw the light at the end of the tunnel that would lead him to his beloved.

He couldn't explain it, but he knew that he loved whoever his angel was. He didn't know how or why. He just loved her like no other.

A few moments later he began to see a light, and hear a faint beeping noise. That was strange. Why were things beeping?

Wasn't he at home on the ranch sleeping in his bed?

Brent's curiosity was what finally helped to get past the last of the fog and go into the light.

He didn't like it much though, it hurt his eyes. There was also sharp pain radiating from his chest and shoulder. Why would he be in pain? He hadn't done anything had he?

He moved his eyes around the room searching for something or someone, but the there wasn't anyone or anything. And the room was strange it had bright yellow walls, and it didn't look anything like his room at home. His room had dark navy blue walls with animal heads and paintings of the Wild West mounted to his walls.

He tried focusing his eyes more, and then it hit him.

He was in a hospital... But why?

He couldn't remember doing anything that would make him need to be there, or anything happening to him for that matter.

Slowly he tried to sit up, but just then a petite blonde woman walked into his room.

"That wouldn't be wise you know. You don't want to bust those stitches in your arm and abdomen."

He couldn't help it he looked at her like she was crazy. But this woman wasn't his angel. She didn't have the right voice.

"Sorry, I should introduce myself. I'm Madison, your nurse. Would you like some water or ice chips you must be parched after your surgery, yesterday?" She smiled kindly at him.

Surgery? He looked over at his shoulder there was a bandage covering it, and his hospital gown was moved slightly to the side to accommodate for it. He noticed a little red on it, and he was confused.

Why was he bleeding, and most of all, why was he in a hospital...?

The nurse looked away from her chart and at him. "Do you know who you are, and how old you are?" she asked him.

Brent nodded his head slowly. "Yeah, Brent Donovan, and I'm twenty-nine."

"Okay, Mr. Donovan, do you know where you are, and what day it is?"

"A hospital," he told her, "but I don't know where or which one." He racked his brain once more, what day was it? "Is it the middle of August?"

Madison stopped and stared at him. "Ugh, no it's not. It's quite the opposite. It's the beginning of December, the fifth to be exact."

He looked at her like she was crazy.

"Do you remember what happened to you?"

"No."

He must have hit his head when he fell, and lost part of his memory. "You're at the hospital in Great Falls, Benefits to be more exact. You were injured in a hunting accident up in Hobson. You were attacked by a mountain lion, and you fell off a cliff and onto a ledge. Your shoulder was fractured into many different pieces, and you received lacerations from the lion. Your lung was also punctured when they found you and had to perform CPR on you. Not to mention the many bruised and broken ribs you have.

"You're a lucky man." She stopped when she realized that he was staring at her. "You have no clue what I'm talking about do you?" He shook his head no at her and she sighed. "I think you received a head injury when you fell making you lose part of your memory."

"Lose part of my memory! I lost four months that's hardly part of my memory!" Brent shouted, and the nurse cringed. He had a temper. "Where's my family."

"The four of them are in the cafeteria eating breakfast. I suppose they'll be back up here in a few minutes."

The four of them? He only had a mom, dad, and sister. Who was this fourth person? He wondered.

Just then a gorgeous tall brunette walked into the room, and Brent was mesmerized. His heart started beating faster, and his palms began to get sweaty.

"Brent!" She smiled. "You're finally awake!" she ran over to him and gave him a gentle hug as to not hurt him.

His angel was hugging him...

*****

I hope you liked it!!!!!!!! We're nearing the end there are probably only a few more chapters left to go and then the epilogue. Then it will be on to The Unexpected Bride. The cover for it is my background on my profile so go check that out if you want to. the song on the side is Cowboys & Angels by Dustin Lynch. I figured that it was fitting since Brent kept calling Anna his angel.

Good news I got accepted to my college, so now all I have to do is call my recruiter and get all of that good stuff set up, and keep getting back into shape before I leave for boot camp!!!! Yay!!! And then after my AIT next year I'll head of to college to study nursing!!! I also just got my cards for being certified in Heartsaver First Aid and Basic Life Support for Healthcare Providers from the American Heart Association today!!! Yay!!!!

This story will still be entered into the Watty Awards!!! It will be under the Original Fiction/Romance once I have it completed. I am not happy that it has to be teen based this year, but I'll give it a whirl, and see if they'll take it. Thanks for reading!!! Please comment and vote!!!

Chapter 25

C hapter 25

Anna was so happy Brent was finally awake. "How are you feeling," she asked him.

He looked at her a little weird. "Like hell, everything hurts." Madison took that as her que to go and get him some pain killers. "Are you my angel? You look like an angel."

"Uh... no. I'm Anna. Do you remember me Brent?"

"No, but your my angel. You kept me company while I was sleeping." He flashed her boyish grin." His face was covered in the beginnings of a beard, and Anna had to admit. He looked quite sexy to her.

"I live on your ranch, Brent. I'm your girlfriend." Anna told him as simply as she could.

He cocked his head to the side. "My girlfriend, but I thought you were my angel?"

Anna couldn't help herself, she giggled. He was just so cute. He looked like a lost puppy. "Nope I'm your girlfriend. We've been seeing each other since the end of September, beginning of October."

"Huh." With his arm that wasn't injured he scratched his forehead in confusion.

The nurse came back into the room and pulled Anna to the side for a chat. "It seems that Brent has short term memory loss. He can't remember anything since the middle of August."

"August? So he doesn't remember me does he?" Anna felt like she'd been punched in the gut. All the air fled from her lungs for a few seconds.

"I'm afraid so. I'm sorry this must be hard to handle. I've seen this multiple times before, and most people make a full recovery in a little while. Although, we won't know for sure until we do some test on him." The nurse smiled at Anna reassuringly. "The good news is that he seems to remember you some."

Anna had a blank look on her face. "Yeah, I guess so."

"One thing that you can do is bring in some of the stuff that he's last seen. Those items could help trigger some memories that might help to return his memory."

Relief flooded Anna, there was a way help him get his memory back. She'd talk to his family and find out where the stuff from his hotel room was currently.

"I'll go talk to the rest of his family, and see what I can scrounge up," Anna told the nurse.

"Sounds like a plan. Now I just need to give him his pain killers." The nurse walked over to Brent and handed him a little cup filled with a couple pills, and then she held the straw up from his water cup so that he could wash them down.

Anna walked into the hallway and called Derek. The phone rang a few times, but then he answered it. "Hey, Derek it's me Anna. I know that you were going to take Brent's stuff back to the ranch, but I was wondering if you could bring everything, but his guns and bows to the hospital."

"Of course, may I ask why though?" Derek thought that it was unusual request. If she would have asked him just for clothes he wouldn't have thought anything of it, but it wasn't just clothes that he would be bringing.

"Brent's not doing very well, he has short term memory loss, and they seem to think that his stuff will bring back all his memories. I don't know what to believe, but if it will help him remember me again, then I'll do anything." Anna told him.

"Oh..." he was silent for a couple seconds. "I'm sorry Anna. I'll be over in a little while with his stuff." Then the line went dead.

Anna went back into Brent's room to find him asleep and snoring because his pain pills had knocked him out. She pulled a chair up next to his bed and waited, she waited for so many things.

For him to wake up, but most of all she waited for him to remember her once again.

Although, she did kind of like being called his, angel.

*****

Later that day everyone had come to terms with Brent's short term memory loss, it had been easier for his family since he still remembered them. He still called Anna his angel, but he was starting to catch himself, and call her by her given name.

Even though Anna had come to term with everything, she still had a pain deep in her chest. Her heart was breaking.

Here was this man that she loved more than her own life, he was in pain from his surgeries and many fracture or broken bone, and he couldn't remember her to save his life. She could tell he wanted to remember her. There was a longing in his eyes every time he looked at her. It was almost as if he knew who she was, but he could remember nothing about her.

It was a little while later when Derek arrived with Brent's things, and he had Luke trailing behind him.

The really sad moment was when Brent remembered Derek, and it'd been over ten years since the last time Brent had seen him while he was conscious.

When Brent heard Derek and Luke enter the room he gave a friendly nod to Luke, and then he studied Derek for a few minutes. "Hey, I remember you. You were called... that's right! Derek the Brace Face."

Derek winced as if he'd been hit in the head, and then Denise went up to Brent and gave him a nice and solid swat to the head.

"Ow!!! What was that for?!" Brent asked his mother.

"You need to be nice young man." She smacked his head again.

"Stop hitting me, that's what they used to call him in high school." He sneered at his mother which ordered him another swat to the head.

"Brent you might just want to stop. All you're doing is moving backwards." His father told him as he chuckled at the sight everyone made.

Brent threw his arm that wasn't in a sling up in the air. "Fine! Fine, I'm sorry. How was that?" he asked everyone.

Denise gave him a small smile. "Good." She then turned towards Derek. "I'm sorry I promise you that I taught him manners. They just never really stuck."

Derek chuckled; he wished his own family was this dysfunctional. "That's alright Mrs. Donovan. I've got your stuff here Brent maybe it will trigger some memories." Derek told him as he set the bags to the side.

Brent smiled sheepishly at everyone and then turned to Derek. "I'm sorry about the whole Brace Face thing."

Denise smacked him one more time over the head.

"OW!!! What was that for?!" Brent asked her again.

"Stop saying those words!" Denise glared at Brent.

Derek patted Brent on his good shoulder. "Don't worry about it. It's alright." He turned and waved to everyone. "Well, I must be going I have to work in the morning. See you all, later."

"You young man need to be more respectful." Denise told him as she poked him in the arm.

Everyone else was just standing by laughing at him.

"I'm sorry momma. My memory must have gotten smacked a little harder than I first thought." He kissed his mom on the cheek, and everyone burst out laughing.

A few hours later everyone began to depart. They needed to get back to the ranch, and Brent needed his beauty sleep.

Anna was the last one to exit the room. She gave Brent a kiss on the forehead and then one on the cheek.

He grabbed her hand before she could walk away. "Thanks for not giving up on me. Most girls would have run for the hills if their guy couldn't remember them." He squeezed her hand.

Anna smiled one her breathtaking smiles at him, and Brent felt his insides turn to mush. He wished that he could remember everything about her. "One thing you'll find out is that I don't give up real easily. I fight for what I want, and what I want is you." With that Anna left Brent to his thoughts.

*****

That night even with all the drugs that they gave Brent, he still couldn't sleep. He sat there racking his brain, and willing memories to come back for a while. But nothing came back to him, and to say that he was frustrated was being nice.

He wanted so badly to remember Anna, but he just couldn't.

Around two a.m. Brent pressed his call light, and had his nighttime nurse bring his bag to him. Maybe looking at his stuff would help him remember.

Two hours later he still could remember nothing. Nothing was triggering a memory, and that's how it went for the next couple of days.

When Brent was finally released from the hospital a few long days later, he was crankier than anyone had ever seen him before, but he was also restless. It seemed like he felt that the key to him remembering was at the ranch. No one knew what to make of it, but instead of questioning it they went along with it.

Anna was beginning to get a little restless as well. She just wanted things to back to the way that they were before. She wanted him to kiss her, and snuggle with her. Most of all she wanted to be able to tell him that she loved him, and have him remember his feeling for her.

Brent had stayed locked in his room since he'd been home. The only time he exited was to go to his office, or to get food. It seemed like he was depressed, and everyone understood why.

Bill and Denise had decided to stay for a little while, or at least until Brent had his memory back.

The real breakthrough came a couple days after Brent had arrived home when he was finally getting around to unpacking his things from his hunting trip. It bothered him that he couldn't remember that trip especially since he'd ended up with a shattered shoulder, a punctured lung and a couple broken ribs.

When Brent was unloading his duffel bag he opened one of the small pockets that he normally couldn't fit anything in, but what he found inside it changed everything.

It was the ring that he'd purchased for Anna. He remembered know, he remembered.

He remembered Cassie putting his name in that magazine, and then hundreds of letters came, but the only one he had bothered to open was Anna's. He remembered sending her a letter back, and then before he knew it she was here.

He remembered when he'd saw her for the first time at the airport. She was absolutely breathtaking. He liked her from the start, but he couldn't do anything about it. He was petrified from fear because of his ex-girlfriend, Leslie.

Then the day in the stable he couldn't help it, she looked so gorgeous, and for a moment he'd lost it and had taken everything out on her. Then she'd gotten lost, and he'd freaked. Already then he knew that he had like Anna, and when he'd found her he'd been so relieved, but they'd both had had smart mouths and had gotten themselves in trouble.

Then everything came crashing down when they'd kissed. It'd been the best one of his life, and then they decided to be friends, but that hadn't worked for him. He didn't want to wait. He wanted it all then, he wanted to be her boyfriend.

Then again he hadn't told her about Leslie yet, but his little sister had had him covered. She'd told Anna and Anna had been understanding. That had helped pave the way for their date in town, and then everything went well from then on. They started dating steadily, but there had been one snag.

Clint had left Cassie. Brent felt his blood boil just thinking about it. Cassie had been lost for a couple of week, but then something had snapped her back to life. Oh, and his parents had visited and then Anna had fainted when they'd been caught kissing.

After Thanksgiving when his parents had left that's when all the problems started. Leslie came back and started creating drama that almost ruined Brent and Anna's relationship. Leslie had broken then down, and had made Anna believe that he was leaving her and going back to Leslie. Which was never going to happen, but Leslie could be manipulative.

That was when he'd decided to go on his trip, Anna needed time and space. So Brent had given it to her, and then he'd ended up like this. The only difference was now he could remember and all he wanted was Anna.

"I love Anna." He whispered to himself.

He had to tell her. He'd told her before he'd left on his trip, but she didn't remember.

He'd go tell her know, and he'd bring the ring with him. Hopefully if everything worked out he'd have a fiancée by the end of the day.

*****

"Hey Chrissie." Anna said, as the phone connected.

"Hey, how have you been? It's been a while since I've talked to you."

"I've been alright I guess." Anna shrugged her shoulders at her remark.

"Are you sure? You don't sound fine. I'm worried about you."

"I'm not okay." Anna broke out into sobs, and just cried her heart out.

"Tell me what's wrong." Chrissie knew that Anna should never have gone to Montana. She should have stayed in New York. This whole thing was just one giant disaster.

"Chrissie he doesn't remember me." Anna cried into the phone. "I don't know what to do anymore. I love him so much." Anna was breaking down, but it had been such a long time since she'd talked to her friend and it felt good.

"Oh, sweetie, didn't they say that his memory would come back soon?" Chrissie questioned her.

"Well, yeah, but it's been a week, and it's been driving me stark raving mad. He doesn't hold me or kiss ne. I mean I understand that he doesn't know what to make of me, but I don't know if I can do this anymore. It hurts so much.

"I love him so much, but how can I be with someone that doesn't re-member me. Maybe I should just come back." That was the last thing she wanted to do, but every day it felt like she was losing the love of her life more and more.

"You know I can't tell you what to do. I think that you need to thing this over for a day or two and then decided." Chrissie wanted Anna to come back, but not if it was going to hurt Anna. "Once you've decided, call me and then we'll go from there, okay?"

That actually sounded like a good idea to Anna. "Alright, I'll call you in a couple days and tell you what I've decided. I miss you, bye Chrissie."

"Bye, Anna. Don't forget to call me I miss you so much." With that the call ended, and Anna was left with a new perspective on thing, or at least until her door opened and a very pissed of Brent walked in.

*****

Brent was right outside Anna's door when he heard her talking to Chrissie. He heard something about her thinking about leaving him, and then the call was over.

She was going to leave him! He couldn't believe this.

Here he was coming to tell her that he loved her and ask her hand in marriage, but not anymore. He wanted her gone. That was what she wanted after all, wasn't it?

Well damn it then he'd let her leave, and he'd even buy her plane ticket.

He opened her door and barged in as if he owned the place, which he did.

Anna was sitting there with a look of shock on her face. "What's going on? Be careful you don't want to tear your stitches." She told him when she noticed a look of discomfort on his face.

"What the hell do you care?!" He roared. "It sounds like you were planning to leave me, anyways."

Anna was caught unawares. He'd heard her conversation with Chrissie.

"Here I was coming to tell you that I remembered you and everything we had, among other things and then I find that you were planning to leave me. Do you know how that makes me feel?" His voice betrayed him, and it broke. He rubbed his good hand over the arm that was in the sling.

Anna had screwed everything up. She should never have called Chrissie, and talked to her about any of that stuff. God, she was so stupid! Stupid! Stupid! Stupid!

"No, no that's not how I meant everything to go. I've made such a mess of things. I love you, so much. But for a while I thought I had lost you." Anna was just about in tears again.

"Well, this time you have. Were you after my money? God, I'd thought that I'd gotten rid of girls like you and Leslie. Only after my money, you make me sick!" Brent was raging mad, he'd thought that he could trust her.

Anna rose from her bed. "Don't you dare accuse me of being like her, you know that I am nothing like her." She got up in his face. "I do love you. I've loved you most of the time I've been here. You money is not why I love you. You are why I love you." She kissed him, but before she could make an attempt to deepen it Brent pushed her away.

"I don't want to leave you Brent," she whispered.

"Well, it's too late. I can't love someone who was going to leave me because I lost my memory and it took me a little while to get it back."

Anna was silently sobbing.

Brent's heart was breaking, too. He didn't want to send her away. He loved her, but he could no longer trust her.

"I'll arrange a plane ticket for tomorrow afternoon to New York. You better have all the stuff you need to take with you packed. I'll have Cassie pack up the rest, and we'll ship it to you.

"I never want to see you again." Brent told her and walked out of her room, and then he too was consumed by tears. He loved her do much, but she'd betrayed him. Her ring was in his pocket, and now he'd never be able to give it to her.

*****

I hope you like it! Sorry for the wait, there will probably only be one maybe two more chapters, and then the epilogue. Please don't hat me everything will work out...

Today has been a crappy day and I'm now sick too, but I'm glad that I could get you all this chapter.

Anyways, the song on the side is great. It's I Can't Love You Back by Easton Corbin. Please vote and comment!!!

Chapter 26

C hapter 26

"Can you give Anna her plane ticket?" Brent asked Cassie the next morning, as he handed her a plane ticket.

The night before, had been a sleepless one for everyone. Brent had tossed and turned which ultimately had hurt his shoulder and stomach more, so he had sat up all night thinking about Anna. He was going to miss her, but he was going to let the thoughts of her betrayal wash away everything else.

It had been a little different for Anna, she'd cried for hours while she'd packed and then she'd ultimately cried herself to sleep. There had been a couple of minutes while she'd been packing where she's called Chrissie to tell her that she'd be coming home. In all honesty Anna didn't know if she was going to be able to leave, she loved him so much.

"No. You're making a huge mistake, and I won't be part of it." Cassie wanted to smack her brother. He just couldn't let Anna leave, but he would listen to the voice of reason.

"Please, Cassie can you just do this for me? And I'm not making a mistake... She betrayed me. She was going to leave me just because I couldn't remember her." Brent was annoyed, and he felt all alone.

"My answer is still no. You will not change my mind." Cassie huffed. "Did you even ask for her side of the story, or did you just go off on a rampage like you always do? Huh? You are one big blubbering idiot."

"Fine! I'll go do it myself, and for your information, little sis I am not an idiot." Brent roared as he exited the living room, heading for the staircase.

He was met with a wall of soft women and he grabbed onto her to steady the both of them. He breathed her scent in and then smiled before he could help himself. The soft women in his arms became still. Brent immediately released her and then he opened up his eyes.

He knew it was Anna who'd been in his arms a moment prior, and seeing her only made it even more real. That was the last time that he was going to get to hold her. He felt a pang in his chest, and then he pushed it to the side and got ahold of himself.

"Would you pay attention to where you're going?" A look of shock came over Anna's face, and then she looked like she wanted to cry. Brent felt a little guilty.

Anna looked down at her hands. "Yeah, sorry." She grabbed ahold of her suitcase which she'd let go of when she'd run into Brent.

Brent grabbed her plane ticket out of his back pocket, and handed it to her. "Here you go."

Panic engulfed Anna. This was all becoming so real, she had to leave know. Her home was once again being ripped from her. A sob tore from her mouth, and Brent did nothing but to stand there watching her. Anna slipped the plane ticked into the messenger bag that was slung across her shoulders.

Anna whipped the tears from her cheeks. "Thank you, I'm so sorry. I never meant to hurt you, Brent."

He just shrugged his shoulders. "Yeah, well you did hurt me, and I can't just forgive you for your betrayal." Brent sighed and rubbed a hand over his face. "One of the hands will take you to the airport. Although, I don't want to know you anymore, I wish you well for the rest of your life." He turned and walked away while Anna started to once again sobbed.

It was only a moment until Cassie was there hugging her, telling her that everything would be okay.

*****

The last of Anna's things were finally packed and she was ready to go. No, that wasn't true. In no way was she ready to leave, but she didn't have a choice now did she.

Anna grabbed her notebook out of her messenger bag and opened it up to a blank page. She was going to write Brent a letter, since he wouldn't listen to her. She had to tell him how sorry she was. Maybe after he read the letter he'd forgive her.

Dear Brent,

I am so sorry for the way that things have ended between us. It makes me even sadder that things have to end at all between us. If it makes any difference I do love you, and I always will. I never meant to make you feel as if though I had betrayed you.

To tell you the truth I don't even know why I called Chrissie. I guess that I was scared about everything that had happened, and I needed someone to talk to. I'd missed Chrissie, and then as I was talking to her. I found myself spilling all my worries out to her. I should never have agreed to go back to New York if things didn't get better. I should have just stuck it out. I knew that you would remember me, but I just broke. I know that there are no excuses for how I betrayed you.

I never wanted your money. I hope that someday you'll realize that all I ever wanted was you, because Brent you're all I have ever wanted. Brent I love you so very much. I hope that one day you can forgive me for everything. For my not believing you when it came to Leslie, but most of all because of how I betrayed you when I got scared.

I'll just stop rambling know. I hope that you'll live a very happy life. I hope you get married and someday have children. You'll be a wonderful father. I realized that soon after I came to Montana. Any woman that you marry will be very lucky, and much loved. I just wish that it was me.

Just ignore that last sentence. I should never have written that, even if it may be true. Good luck Brent, and just remember that I love you and that I'm sorry.

With much love,

Anna Douglas

She folded the letter, and put it in an envelope. Anna signed Brent's name across the top of it and left it on her nightstand. For some reason she knew that there was no need for her to slip it under his door, he'd find it here in her old room soon enough. After all he did have to send the rest of her things back to her, which meant that he would have to enter her room.

Anna grabbed her messenger bag as slung it over her shoulders, and then she grabbed her suitcase. As she walked over to the door to exit she turned around one more time to just take everything in one last time.

This whole thing was so bitter sweet. As she looked at her room one last time she sent up a silent prayer that maybe, just maybe Brent would come after her. That he wouldn't just let her go, but she knew that that was just wishful thinking. He wouldn't come after her that wasn't who he was, he'd let her go. After all he had no reason to come after him, she'd betrayed him when he'd needed her most.

Anna brushed away the lone tear that tricked down her face, as she exited her old room, and then shut the door behind her.

She waked down the hallway to the staircase while she lugged her suitcase behind her. Memories assaulted her, but she kept walking. Thinking about those memories would just make it even harder than it already was for her to leave.

Lugging her suitcase down the stairs was bit of a chore, but Anna just was able to get to the bottom of the stairs rather easily. As Anna turned to the right so that she could go to the living room she ended up running into someone.

Oh she knew who it was. Of course it just had to be Brent.

He grabbed ahold of her to help steady them so that they wouldn't fall. His face was right by her neck, and Anna couldn't help it. She shivered just a little bit.

When Brent let go of her she felt the loss of his warmth, and tears flooded her eyes when she realized that that was the last time Brent would hold her.

"Would you pay attention to where you're going?" The need to cry overcame her even more when she was met with Brent's harsh words.

She looked immediately down at her hand while she muttered a hushed, "sorry" to him. She grabbed her suitcase once again.

When she looked back up from grabbing her suitcase Brent was holding out a plane ticket to her. "Here you go."

Anna felt like screaming. She didn't want to leave, and then she became overcome with panic. She let a sob loose, but no one comforted her, but Anna hadn't expected Brent to hug her. She then took the ticket from him and put it up in her bag.

"Thank you. I'm sorry." She paused, but Brent didn't notice. "I never meant to hurt you."

"Yeah, well you did hurt me, and I can't just forgive you for your betrayal." Anna watched as he ran a hand over his face. . "One of the hands will take you to the airport. Although, I don't want to know you anymore, I wish you well for the rest of your life."

Brent then walked away, and it was only moments before Anna began crying, but before she knew it Cassie was there holding her.

"I'm so sorry, Anna. I tried to make him see the light, but my brother is as stubborn as they come. There are a couple more things that I would like to call him, but I think that I refrain from doing so." Cassie hugged Anna little tighter, and then she began to release Anna when she noticed that her cries had begun to stop.

"Cassie, what am I going to without you, you're like a sister to me. I'm going to miss you so very much, along with," Anna pointed at Cassie's slightly pooched stomach, but you wouldn't notice it unless you knew that Cassie was pregnant, "this little guy. Please promise that we'll call, Skype, and visit each other whenever we can. I couldn't stand to lose you, too."

"You won't lose me. I'll always be there for you if you ever need anything. It just makes me sad that you'll never truly be my sister." Cassie sighed, but then smiled at Anna. "You would truly have made my brother a wonderful wife."

"I wish that it could have happened, but he'll find someone else to make him happy, and hopefully someday I will, too." Anna tried to smile, but there was no way that that was going to happen write then.

"You will Anna, you'll meet someone amazing and they'll make you extremely happy. And then you'll be the one having to keep me in the loop when you have children." Cassie hugged her once more. "As for my brother, well right now I don't give a damn what happens to him. I'm so pissed off at the way he's acting."

"Don't be too mad at him, he's not the only one to blame. I am, too." Anna would forever feel guilty over everything that had happened.

"I'm sorry Anna. We all have moments of weakness, but unfortunately Brent went too far when you had yours."

"Thanks, Cass. I think I'm going to go and say goodbye to Cupid, and the other horses. I'm going to miss my boy." Anna's lip wobbled a little bit.

"Don't worry I'll take good care of him. I know how much you love that horse." She patted Anna on the arm. "Go see him one last time." She looked down at her watch. "You've got about fifteen minutes until you have to leave."

"Thanks, Cass." Anna hugged her one more time, and then she went and put her bags in the living room before she exited the house for the barn.

Saying goodbye to Cupid and all of the hands was hard. Cupid had basically become a best friend to Anna in the short time she'd been in Montana, and the hands, well they were all like close friends on brothers to her.

Once she was done saying goodbye, Anna went back to the house to grab her stuff. Cassie was waiting for her and she gave her one last hug.

"Goodbye Anna and good luck." Cassie told her.

"Thank Cass, you too." With that she had to leave. She took her things and exited the house the waiting truck for her. As she got into the truck she knew that her life would never be the same.

*****

Brent had been watching from his window upstairs as Anna had left, and it had just about damn near broken his heart apart. Although, it had brought him down to his knees as he watched the truck drive away with Anna in it. He'd fallen apart when he'd realized that she really was gone, but he couldn't go after her. He just couldn't.

The sense of betrayal was just too much. He couldn't be with someone that would betray him when they knew about his past.

He stayed on the floor of his room for a good half an hour after Anna had left. When he got up he felt lost and alone. He never knew that losing one's only true love could hurt this bad.

Somehow he found the nerve to leave his room, but he didn't know where he was going until he found himself standing outside of Anna's room.

What was he doing? It's not like if he opened that door she would be standing there waiting for him, and then everything would be okay.

He knew that he wasn't going to find anything but boxes in her room, but Brent couldn't help it he had to go in there. The closure that Brent needed was waiting in Anna's room.

The door creaked when he opened it and instantly his nose was assaulted by Anna's scent. She was gone, yet her scent still lingered just about everywhere he went.

When he walked into her room he went over to the bed and sat down. She'd taken off her own bedding set, and had put the original set back on the bed. He remembered how he'd spent the night sleeping in this bed with her before he'd left on his hunting trip.

He remembered how soft she had felt in his arms, how perfectly they had fit together. He missed her so much. He'd been so stupid to let her go.

He had let his everything go. The woman that he hoped he would one day marry. The woman that he had hoped would one day bear his children.

He'd just let her go.

And for what some stupid reason that she'd betrayed him. What a joke. He was such a joke.

She had never really betrayed him. He'd gotten scared at the thought of losing her, but instead he'd pushed her away on his own. He was so stupid and he realized that now, but now was too late.

She probably didn't even look back or miss him, and it was his entire fault. If only he'd listened to her things would be different.

An envelope on Anna's bedside table got Brent's attention and when he looked at it even closer it had his name scrawled across the top of it.

Intrigued he picked up the letter, and opened it. What he read changed everything.

She did love him. She still wanted him. He read it again to make sure that his mind wasn't playing a trick on him.

He couldn't believe it. If what he had read was true then she didn't want to leave. She wanted to stay here with him.

He had to do something. He had to find her. He had to get her back.

She wanted to marry him. She wanted to have his children. She wanted exactly what he wanted, and one thing became extremely real to him.

He had to find here and get her back.

Brent high tailed it out of Anna's room, and then went to his own. When he opened up the door to his room, he went over to his dresser. He opened up the top drawer and found the box that contained Anna's wring sitting there. Brent snatched it up, grabbed the keys to his truck and then he ran downstairs.

Cassie was watching him from the living room when he got downstairs. "What are you doing Brent?" she questioned him.

He was breathing hard from running around the house. He pulled the letter from Anna out of his pocket, and held it up. "She still wants me. Anna wants me even though I've been terrible to her. I-I have to get her back." He pulled his leys from his pocket and began to take off.

"Hold on!" Cassie yelled after him. "You can't drive one handed. Let me drive you."

Brent looked at his arm and sighed. He'd forgotten that one of his arms was still in a cast. "Damn it! I completely forgot. Thanks Cass. Now let's hurry!"

He grabbed Cassie's arm and practically drug her out to his truck, and then he threw his keys at Cassie.

Cassie couldn't help it she laughed at him when she jumped up into the truck. "No problem, Brent. I'm just glad you finally came to your senses." She smiled over at him.

*****

Two hours later Cassie and Brent pulled up in front of the airport, and right as Cassie stopped the car Brent hopped out.

"Thanks Cassie you are the best!" Brent took off itowards the airport.

"You're welcome, Brent just remember that. Oh, and I wouldn't mind if you named your first born after me!" Cassie giggled a little at that.

Brent turned back around. "Cassie you are the best, but don't count on it."

He turned back around and ran into the airport, straight to the screens that displayed the departure times. He scanned it for flight 841 to New York City, New York.

He still had ten minutes until her flight boarded, but it was on the other side of the airport. He'd have to take the train and get through security. It'd be a miracle if he made it in time, but he was going to try.

Brent took off running to the train that would take him to the terminal where Anna was.

When he stepped on the train there was an old man standing next to him.

"Are you in a hurry son?" the hold man asked him. He looked to be in his early seventies with a slightly rounded belly.

Brent was tapping his cowboy booted foot in anticipation, and he hadn't even realized it. He stopped and nodded at the man. "Yes, sir."

"Well, what's got you running around like a damn chicken with his head cut off." He man chuckled, and so did Brent.

"I've got to go and get my girl back." There was a grin spreading Brent's face.

"So you screwed up, son?" He said it as a question, but it was more of a statement.

"Yes sir, but I'm going to find her, apologize, and hopefully get her back."

"You know what." The old man paused a moment. "You're just like me when I was your age. I almost lost my Mary to my damn stubbornness, too." He chuckled.

"Is that so?" Brent asked him with a smile.

"It is." The man went told him the story, and Brent found himself enjoying it. It helped get his mind off of what he was about to do.

When the trained dinged a couple minutes later, Brent got off, and waved goodbye to the man. "I really enjoyed our chat, thanks for the talk."

"No problem, son. Now go and get that girl of yours." The man patted his back, and then walked in the opposite direction as Brent.

"Thanks!" Brent yelled to the man. He turned around and nodded his head to Brent.

Brent took off running towards, Anna's gate, but he was stopped at the security checkpoint at the front of the terminal.

When he went through the metal detector, it beeped and a TSA lady took him off to the side to be checked with a hand wand.

Brent groaned. How could this be happening, he was so close…!

"Ma'am I know you need to do this, but can you please hurry. My girl is getting on a plane, and I have to go and find her." Brent pleaded with the woman.

"I've heard that a thousand times, but it still doesn't change the fact that I still have to make sure that you're not a danger to anyone." The women couldn't help, but giggle. Here was another guy that had gotten in trouble with his lady. Men were so daft.

A few minutes later Brent was tapping his foot rapidly. "Am I done know?"

You are. Good luck with your lady."

That was all Brent needed he took off at a run towards the gate where Anna's plane was taking off from. He looked at his watch, he had one more minute, and there was still have a terminal till he would reach her gate.

When he got to Anna's gate he looked around for her, and the he saw her. She was right about to walk through the door that would lead her to the plane that would end up taking her away from him.

"Anna!" Brent bellowed, but she didn't turn around. "Anna! It's me Brent! I love you!!!"

That got Anna's attention—but it also got everyone else's attention—and she turned around, scanning the crowd in the terminal for his face.

He ran over towards her. "Anna," he said a couple of feet from her.

She looked at him as if he was a mirage. Like she couldn't believe that he was really there. "Brent," she whispered.

"Yeah, Anna it's me." Anna squealed and jumped into his arms, and promptly kissed him on the mouth.

When she broke away she sighed, and laid her head on Brent's shoulder. "I thought I'd lost you."

Brent sighed. "Oh, Anna you could never loose me. I've been such a jerk to you, and I'm so sorry. I know that you're not Leslie, and I'm sorry that I let my fears get in the way of us." Brent bent his head down and kissed her forehead lovingly.

Anna lifted her head to his. "I'm sorry, too. I should never have called Chrissie like that. I was scared that you weren't going to remember me, and that you wouldn't want me. I should never have let my fears get the better of me. Especially when I knew that you would remember me again someday."

"Now that we've gotten that out of the way..." Brent smiled at her. "I love you, Anna and I never want to lose you again."

Anna smiled at him. "Me neither." She pecked him on the lips.

He set her on her feet. Brent grabbed the ring box out of the breast pocket on his western shirt, and then he kneeled down in front of her.

He grabbed her hands. "Anna, I love you."

Anna smiled, and giggled. "I love you, too."

Brent stuttered a little after Anna had told him that she loved him, but he continued on. "I think I've loved you for a long time, but I was just too stubborn to realize it." He pulled her letter out of his pocket. "I want you want to. I want to marry you, and have children with you. I want to live on the ranch with you, but most of all I want to grow old loving you until my very last day." Anna's eyes filled with tears of happiness.

"Will you do me the honor of becoming my wife, my mail order bride?" Anna nodded her head at him.

"Yes, a million times yes." Anna pulled him up to her face, and kissed him while the crowd behind them cheered. She relished in feeling of being with the man of her dreams.

When she peeled herself away from him she sighed. "I love you so much, Brent."

He pecked her on the lips. "I love you, too." He pulled her to his chest and held her tight, or at least as well as he could with his injured arm. "Now how soon can we start on those babies?"

Anna laughed, and kissed him on the lips. "Whenever you'd like."

words! It's so long!!! Please vote and comment!!!

Epilogue

- -

E pilogue

Six years later

"How was your ride," Anna asked her husband as he walked up to their house holding their five year old daughter in his arms.

"It was great wasn't it?" He looked at their daughter, Sophie. She was the spitting image of her mother with her brown hair, and the shape of her face, but she had Brent's gray eyes.

"It was, daddy. I love to ride my pony." Sophie smiled at her parents.

"I know you do sweet pea." Brent kissed Sophie on hair, and then set her down. The girl ran straight over to her mother, whom was sitting in one of the rocking chairs on the porch, holding her little brother, Mason.

"Hi, Mason." The toddler giggled and grabbed Sophie's brown locks.

"Mason." Anna scolded him, and he immediately let go of Sophie's hair, but Anna couldn't be mad at him. He was only one, and he was still learning what was right and wrong. He too was a mix of both his parent's. Mason had Anna's brown hair, and Brent's gray eyes.

Brent walked over to Anna and gave her a sweet kiss on her lips. "Where's Easton?"

"Oh, he's over at Cassie's playing with her son. He should be home in an hour or so." Anna told Brent, Easton was their four year old bucket of joy, and he just so happened to be best friends with Cassie's little boy. Easton looked exactly like his father. He was going to be quite the looker someday when he got older just like his father.

"Let's go inside it's getting a little chilly." Brent spoke up shivering a little when the chill of November caused him to shiver. He grabbed Mason from Anna's arms.

"I think that that sounds like capitol idea." She smiled at him as she got up from the rocking chair on the porch.

They all walked inside together. Mason cooed in Brent's arms and Sophie talked Anna's ear off. This was her family and she loved them all/ the only thing that would have made the moment better was if Easton would have been back from Cassie's.

Anna and Brent were married five months after that faithful day at the airport. Since Anna was still not on speaking terms with her family, Bill walked her down the aisle to a very nervous Brent.

It had been one of the best days of her life. It was right up there with the births of her three children.

Although, Brent and Anna's relationship had started out rocky they made the best of every bad situation. And if there was ever anything that they learned, it was for them to not go to bed angry. They'd learned that lesson from Brent's little hunting trip.

Denise and Bill were the greatest grandparents imaginable. They spoiled their grandchildren into oblivion, but they couldn't be happier. Although, they hadn't been so happy when Cassie had told them that she was preg- nant, and for that matter Brent wasn't too happy either. It wasn't that they didn't want her to have a baby it was more of an, I want you to be married, and I don't want the father of your baby to be God knows where. But that's a story for another time.

They didn't started having babies right away, but when the wedding rolled around Anna was two months pregnant with, whom they later found out was a little girl. They chose to name their little girl Sophie, much to Cassie's chagrin.

For their honeymoon they went on a European tour for a month because Anna had always wanted to see all of Europe. Brent had to admit that he'd enjoyed it as well. There was so much history and so many romantic places to go in Europe. Oh, and did he take advantage of the romantic places, if Anna hadn't already been pregnant then she surely would have been by the end of their honeymoon.

Brent wasn't disappointed that they were having a girl first, he was just happy that he'd have his own little Anna. If there was one thing that he knew for sure it was that no boy was going to go near his little girl, and well if one tried to date her—let's just say Brent had a very shiny shotgun for that situation. He hadn't thought about Sophie marrying anyone because he was never going to let that happen.

Oh, but it did. When Sophie was seventeen she graduated from high school and then attended the University of Montana at Bozeman to study nursing where she met her future husband and the father of her children. Brent had a conniption, but when he realized how happy the young man made his Sophie. When Sophie was twenty-three she got married on her parents ranch to 2nd Lieutenant Jeremy Folsom, and then she lived her life traipsing all over the world working in Army hospitals as nurse with her husband, and two children.

Well, Easton he took over the ranch and had all the ladies chasing after him. He became quite the player, always moving from one girl to another, never staying long enough to get to know a girl. That was until he got tied up by a girl from an abusive past. She brought out the protectiveness in Easton and turned his life around. Much to Easton's chagrin they had two little girls—he didn't know what to do with them, but he was extremely protective over them—and twin boys that were as mischievous as their father.

As for Mason was quite the nervous Nelly not to mention that he was so quiet. He couldn't talk to girls to save his life. Anna thought it was endearing, but sometimes Brent didn't know how to raise Mason. Mason played sports, but he tended to stay home on the weekends studying and riding his mare, Merlin. He was quiet the fan of history, but he went on to study business at the University of Wyoming. Then he went back home to Montana and opened up the biggest horse breeding ranch with the knowledge he'd learned growing up. Mason thought he'd be alone forever, but then he hired a female horse trainer, and let's just say it was love at first sight. They had three little girls, and one little boy.

Anna confided her love of writing with Brent, and he supported her with her writing. Brent was always the first to read every single one of her manuscripts. Shortly after they had Sophie, Anna sold her first manuscript, and kept writing while she raised their three children. By the time all of the kids where in high school Anna was at the top of the New York's Best Seller list. Anna Donovan became an extremely well-known name in America. Some of her books were even adapted into films, but Anna never lost sight of what was important to her, her family. She never missed a holiday or a birthday because of a book tour.

While Anna's career soared so did the ranch it began just about doubling its proceeds every single year. It became the largest and most profitable ranch in all of Montana. Brent had made the ranch into everything that he'd ever dreamed of in his whole life, and it was all because he had a loving wife and wonderful children by his side the whole time.

As for Chrissie, Cassie, and Jess their futures were to be told on their own. Each one had its own joy and problems.

That night after Anna and Brent had put the Kids to bed, they were both sitting up in bed. Anna was working on her next manuscript, and Brent was reading a cattleman's magazine.

Anna saved her work, closed the laptop and then set it on her night stand. She rolled over and grabbed the magazine from Brent's hands and then she threw it across the room.

Their love never faltered. Yes they had problems, but they never let them get in the way of their love. They grew old together and they loved one another until their last days, and even beyond them. It had never mattered that Anna was practically a mail order bride. He just relished in the feeling that she had chosen to stay with him.

Brent looked up startled from Anna's actions, but then he grinned when he saw the look of hunger on Anna's face.

"Well, well. What do you have planned for tonight?" Brent rolled over on top of Anna.

"All the kids are in bed and…" she ran her finger over Bren's bare chest and he smiled. "I thought that maybe we could have an adventure… exploring each other." She smiled wickedly at him.

"Well that depends. How far does this adventure go for, and for how long?" He began to strip the lace camisole from her shoulders.

"As long and as far as you want it to go," she whispered as she leaned her lips up to meet his.

He kissed her passionately on the mouth. "Now that's an offer that I just can't refuse." He growled into Anna's ear and she shivered while she giggled.

She loved it when he growled into her ear. "I love you."

Brent smiled down at her. "And I love you more than you'll ever know." Brent looked away and then back at Anna. "Thank you," he whispered.

"For what?" Anna asked him curiously.

"You gave me everything that I could ever have dreamed of. You gave me our three beautiful children, you stayed here and most of all for loving me. I'm truly the luckiest man in the whole world." He smiled at her and kissed right where her heart would be.

"It was my pleasure." Anna smiled lovingly up at him.

The End—ish